"I g... ... ...
you'... ...
and fou... ...
Dominic obse...

"That's ridiculous...." Jaime tried to sound indignant.

"Is it?" He surveyed her tense figure without remorse. "You don't approve of my— friendship with my stepmother, do you?"

"We agreed to leave your or private affairs alone."

"Affairs?" Dominic's tone mocked her. "What an emotive word that is." He moved a little closer to her. "Have you had many affairs, Jaime? Are you perhaps an expert on what goes on? I can't believe I'm the first man to be fascinated by those intriguing features of yours...."

ANNE MATHER began writing when she was a child, progressing through torrid teenage romances to the kind of adult romances she likes to read. She's married, with two children, and she lives in the north of England. After writing, she enjoys reading, driving and traveling to different places to find settings for new novels. She considers herself very lucky to do something that she not only enjoys, but also gets paid for.

Anne Mather has over one hundred and twenty-five novels published in Harlequin Presents and consistently appears on bestseller lists, including the *New York Times.* Her latest single-title release, *Dangerous Temptation,* is available from MIRA Books.

Books by Anne Mather

Anne Mather

Shattered Illusions

Harlequin Books

TORONTO • NEW YORK • LONDON
AMSTERDAM • PARIS • SYDNEY • HAMBURG
STOCKHOLM • ATHENS • TOKYO • MILAN
MADRID • WARSAW • BUDAPEST • AUCKLAND

ISBN 0-373-11911-9

SHATTERED ILLUSIONS

First North American Publication 1997.

Copyright © 1997 by Anne Mather.

This edition published by arrangement with Harlequin Books S.A.

® and TM are trademarks of the publisher. Trademarks indicated with
® are registered in the United States Patent and Trademark Office, the
Canadian Trade Marks Office and in other countries.

Printed in U.S.A.

CHAPTER ONE

SHE shouldn't have come.

The feeling grew stronger every minute she was kept waiting in this beautiful room, which was nothing like any office she had ever imagined.

But office it was, despite the drifting clouds of chiffon at the long windows. A place where Catriona Redding wrote her very successful novels, regardless of the famous paintings that looked down from the silk-hung walls.

Jaime drew a steadying breath.

The desk alone must have cost a small fortune. A singular slab of polished granite, its surface was strewn with the evidence of Catriona Redding's profession. Files, books, a veritable plethora of pens and pencils; Jaime already knew that she preferred to write her books in longhand, and who could blame her? Sitting in this room, which reflected the light of the huge outdoor pool that flanked it, with the sweep of Copperhead Bay beyond, the clatter of keys would have been an intrusion, even from the computer that Jaime would be expected to employ.

If she was taken on for the probationary two weeks...

And she was by no means certain that she would be. Although she had passed the preliminary interview with Catriona Redding's agent in London, she had still to meet the woman herself, had still to be approved by her proposed employer. It had been made clear to her from the outset that Catriona Redding would make the final decision. For all she was here in Bermuda, the job still hung in the balance.

She cast another look about her, wondering if leaving her here in this impressive apartment was intended to intimidate her. She knew so little about the woman she had come here to meet, and the longer she remained in isolation, the more doubtful about her own motives she became.

What was she doing here? she asked herself. What did she hope to achieve? Did she really want to be Catriona Redding's secretary, even briefly? She was a lecturer in English, for heaven's sake. It was years since she'd taken orders from anyone.

She knew the obvious answer, of course. She wanted to meet Catriona Redding. She wanted to meet her, and get to know her in an unthreatening capacity, to try and find out why she'd done what she had. It had seemed the easiest—if not the wisest—way of achieving her ambitions, without embarrassing either herself or Catriona Redding. If she was taken on, she'd worry about her choices then. For now, she was content to take one day at a time.

Or she had been until a rather snooty housekeeper had shown her into Catriona Redding's study...

The instructions she had been given in London had been explicit. She was to regard this interview—at Catriona Redding's luxury estate in Bermuda—as a preliminary to being given two weeks' probationary tenure. In consequence, she had been advised to bring her immediate needs with her, and should the position be made permanent she should make arrangements for the rest of her belongings to be sent on.

Which had seemed reasonable enough, and Jaime had quite enjoyed the unfamiliar trip across the Atlantic. She'd always liked flying, and her seat in the British Airways jet had been very comfortable. Had she not had a germ of apprehension beavering away in the pit of her stomach, she might have been able to appreciate the trip for its own sake. She had never crossed the Atlantic before, and although Bermuda was not a West Indian island it was situated nearer to the American continent than anywhere else.

And that was probably why she was feeling so uneasy now, she decided. The holidays she'd taken in Europe had not prepared her for the effects of jet lag, and although it was a sunny evening here in Bermuda her body clock was telling her it was already after eleven. She was tired. That was why so many doubts were assailing her. When she'd had a good night's sleep, she'd feel much more optimistic.

But before that happened...

A sudden splash, as if of an object striking water, alerted her to the fact that someone was using the pool outside. The patio windows were slightly ajar, as witness the billowing curtains, but even if she had not been able to hear the rippling water she'd have guessed what was happening by the patterns spreading on the ceiling above her head.

She was tempted to get up and see who it was. But the anxiety—fear—that it might be Catriona Redding kept her anchored to her seat. Besides, she did not want to be caught spying on whoever might be using the pool. She had to remember she was here for an interview, and, as such, she would be unwise to risk losing the job out of curiosity.

All the same, her eyes were drawn in that direction, and she felt a twinge of envy for whoever had the right to cool off in that way. For all the room was air-conditioned, she could feel the draught of warm air coming in through the crack in the windows, and her nerves were working overtime to send an unpleasant trickle of perspiration down her spine.

A shadow moved beyond the windows, and she realised the swimmer had emerged from the pool. She saw the silhouette of a man, tall and dark, moving with a lithe grace across the tiled apron. His back was to her, for which she was grateful, for when he bent to lift a towel from one of the chairs that faced the water she was almost sure he was naked.

Her mouth dried instantly. Whoever he was, he was obviously someone Catriona Redding knew well. She blinked. It was something that had not occurred to her. That the woman might be involved with someone else. Which was foolish, she acknowledged impatiently. Successful women could have their pick of admirers.

All the same, Catriona Redding had to be fifty, if she was a day, and the man who had drawn Jaime's eyes appeared to be in the prime of his life. Though she couldn't really tell through the drifting veils of chiffon. It was just an impression she had received from the casual indolence of his stride.

She swallowed uneasily, hoping that, whoever he was, he wouldn't decide to enter the house through the study's inviting windows. Could she get up and close them before he noticed? Would he think she'd been spying on him, if he glimpsed her through the glass? She didn't know why she had such a strong compulsion to avoid a complete stranger, but she breathed a little more freely when he moved away.

Her relief at this escape almost overshadowed the sudden opening of the door. But the reminder of why she was here brought her automatically to her feet, and she was already schooling her features when Catriona Redding turned to face her.

'Miss Harris?' The name could mean nothing to her, and the hand she held out to Jaime was as cool and impersonal as she could have expected. Slim fingers, their elegance enhanced by several gold rings—none of them a wedding ring—gripped Jaime's fingers briefly. 'Please sit down, Miss Harris,' she instructed smoothly, seating herself in the grey leather chair across the desk. 'Did you have a pleasant journey?'

Jaime struggled to find her tongue. She hadn't expected to be so affected by this first meeting, and it was galling to feel as nervous as she did. She was an honours graduate, for God's sake. For the past five years she had been lecturing to students who should have been far more intimidating than one woman. But the fact remained she was tongue-tied, as much by Catriona Redding's appearance as anything else.

The woman was quite simply stunning. Her silken cap of silvery blonde hair, tinted perhaps, framed a face that showed little evidence of its years. Dark blue eyes, between sooty lashes, were spaced wide above well-marked cheekbones. A delicately shaped nose set off a mouth that was full-lipped without being exactly generous. And her skin was smooth and unblemished, and only lightly touched with a golden tan.

Jaime didn't quite know what she had expected, or quite why she was as surprised as she was. She'd seen Catriona Redding's picture on the jackets of her books, so she should have been prepared for this. But the reality was so much more shocking than the image had ever been.

'Is something wrong?'

Jaime's hands clenched in her lap. Pull yourself together, she chided herself angrily. Do you want her to think you're naive as well as stupid?

'I'm sorry,' she said hurriedly, hoping she didn't sound too sycophantic. 'It's just such a—a thrill—for me, meeting you in the flesh. I've—read all your books, Miss Redding.' That, at least, was true. 'I'm a great admirer of your work.'

Was she?

'You are?' Apparently the other woman accepted this without question. A wintry smile appeared. 'Do you have a favourite? I'm always interested to hear which books strike a chord with my readers.'

Jaime swallowed. For a moment her mind went blank, and she couldn't remember even one of the titles. But then rationality returned, and she found what she was looking for. Even if it was difficult to be objective when she'd read all twenty books in less than a month.

'I—I think I enjoyed *Heartless* best,' she answered, wondering if her choice, which had been made at random, possessed some hidden meaning she was unaware of. After all, her father would probably say the title was appropriate, but she didn't want to think of Robert Michaels right now.

Thankfully, her answer seemed to satisfy her would-be employer, and she made some deprecatory comment that allowed Jaime a little more time to study her appearance. If she hadn't known better, she'd have guessed that Catriona Redding was in her late thirties. There was an air of agelessness about her that was deliberately enhanced by the rather severely tailored suit she was wearing.

'I believe you've been living in London, Miss Harris,' she prompted now, and Jaime endeavoured to keep her mind on why she was supposed to be here. Why she was here, dammit, she reminded herself fiercely. It wouldn't do to appear too overwhelmed at the prospect of working with the famous author.

'Um—yes,' she replied, aware that she was being given a penetrating appraisal in her turn. 'I—er—I've been working as a research assistant at the university.'

'So I see.' Catriona consulted the file she had taken from the pile on her desk. 'Impressive qualifications for someone who wants to work as my secretary.' She lifted her head. 'Do you mind telling me why you want this job?'

Jaime drew a breath, and started on the explanation she had devised for just this situation. 'I've been restless for some time,' she said, which was also true. 'And, before I got my degree, I took time out to get some secretarial qualifications, and worked for nine months as a secretary in a small publishing house. That—that was what first inspired my interest in your books, Miss Redding. One of the girls I worked with lent me *Harvest Moon*, and—and I've been a fan ever since.'

'And this—interest in my work encouraged you to give up your position at the university?'

Catriona sounded sceptical, and Jaime couldn't altogether blame her.

'Partly,' she answered carefully. 'But, as I said before, I was already dissatisfied with my job. Researching ancient languages can become boring, Miss Redding. I was looking for something new, and when I saw your advertisement it seemed like an amazing coincidence.'

'I see.'

Catriona continued to regard her with that faint air of suspicion, and Jaime had to control the impulse to check that her hair was still neatly confined in its braid or that her lipstick wasn't smudged. There was no way this woman could know that she had not been employed as a research assistant, she assured herself. Her superior at the college was a friend, and it had only meant twisting his words a little.

'So tell me about yourself,' Catriona suggested at last. 'My agent dealt with your qualifications, and the salary that's on offer. I want to know a few personal details, Miss Harris. Tell me about your family.'

Jaime moistened her lips. 'I don't have a family, Miss Redding.' Then, taking a chance, she said, 'My father died a few months ago, and I have no other close relations.'

'No husband?' Catriona consulted her notes again. 'I see from your application that you're almost thirty, Miss Harris. Aren't you interested in getting married?'

'Not at present.'

Jaime wasn't at all convinced that such a question was warranted. Just because Catriona Redding wrote passionate novels about relationships between the sexes, that did not give her the right to probe the psyches of her employees. If she had been applying for this job in a purely impersonal capacity, she would have resented it. As it was, she put it down to Catriona's curiosity and nothing else.

'But you do want to get married one day?' the woman was asking now, and Jaime wondered what she was implying. Did she want some committed career woman, who wouldn't waste a second glance on a man? Or was there some other reason for her interest?

'Maybe,' she conceded at last. And then, because something more was needed, she added, 'My work didn't leave a lot of time for socialising.'

Catriona frowned. 'I hope you don't see this job as a sinecure, Miss Harris. That is to say, working for me will not be an easy ride. I tend to work long hours without a break, and my personal deadlines are demanding, to say the least.'

'I'm not looking for an easy option, Miss Redding,' Jaime assured her hurriedly. 'If you suspect that the prospect of working here, in such idyllic surroundings, was the main reason I applied for this job, you couldn't be more wrong. Of course, it's more attractive than— than where I used to work, but I'm not overawed by my surroundings. If you give me an opportunity to prove myself, I'm sure you won't be disappointed.'

'So you haven't come here looking for a wealthy husband, Miss Harris?' And before Jaime could voice her indignation she went on, 'It's not been unknown. My last assistant made quite a nuisance of herself, and I'm afraid I had to dismiss her.' She paused. 'But you look a much more—sensible girl. Kristin was a flirt, and far too concerned with her own appearance.'

Which was as good as saying that she was unattractive, and therefore no competition, thought Jaime drily. How could someone who wrote such sensitive prose be so insensitive herself? She caught her upper lip between her teeth. If she wasn't careful, she'd start by disliking the woman. This was going to be so much harder than she'd thought.

'I'm not interested in finding a husband, Miss Redding,' she assured her firmly. 'I think I can safely say you will not have to fire me on those terms. I simply want a change of—focus. As I said in my application, I should very much like to work with you.'

The sincerity in her tone was convincing—as well it should be, reflected Jaime, with an inner smile. If Catriona Redding had lived in the wilds of Alaska or the slums of Calcutta, she would have been just as keen to work for her. But even she drew back from admitting that.

'Very well.' Catriona rose from her seat, and walked with unhurried grace to the long windows. Drawing the filmy curtain aside, she looked out on the pool area outside. Whatever she saw beyond the windows seemed to please her, for when she turned back to Jaime she was wearing a much more indulgent expression. 'Very well,' she said again. 'As my agent will have informed you, I'm prepared to offer a two-week trial, if that's agreeable to you. Naturally, you will be given the same privilege.' Her smile intimated how generous the offer was. 'We'll soon find out if we—suit one another.' She paused. 'All right?'

She'd done it.

Jaime's breath left her lungs in a rush. 'All right,' she echoed, amazed to hear that her voice sounded so normal. And then, because she felt it was expected of her, she said, 'Thank you.'

'Good.' Catriona walked back to her desk and pressed a button on the intercom. 'Sophie?' She cast a look at Jaime as she waited. 'Sophie's my housekeeper,' she explained. And then, as the woman answered, she said, 'Yes, Sophie. I've decided to offer Miss—um—Harris the job. She'll be starting work tomorrow. Can you come and show her to her apartments, please?'

* * *

Her rooms were situated in a kind of annexe. It was attached to the main house by means of a vine-hung walkway, which even at this hour of the evening was fragrant with the scent of the pale pink flowers that grew there. The pool she had glimpsed earlier was just visible beyond the white-painted wall of the house, and from a dusk-shaded cupola came the drowsy sound of doves.

Idyllic surroundings indeed, she reflected, still basking in the glow of her success. The only fly in her particular ointment was the housekeeper, Sophie, who still maintained the air of superiority she'd adopted when she'd first shown Jaime into the house.

The door to her apartments had a key, she noticed with some relief, but it wasn't locked, and Sophie thrust it open without ceremony. 'I'm sure you'll find you have everything you need here,' she declared, using the switch by the door to turn on several lamps. 'Miss Spencer had no complaints. She was very happy here.'

'Was she?'

Jaime was beginning to get an inkling as to why Sophie resented her. Evidently, this Miss Spencer was the Kristin Catriona Redding had spoken of so disparagingly, but Sophie clearly considered that she should still have the job.

Deciding there was no point in pursuing the matter, Jaime surveyed the living room they had entered with real pleasure. 'Did you do this, Sophie?' she asked, indicating an arrangement of hibiscus and bird of paradise flowers that occupied a prominent position on a low table. Dark green waxy leaves cradled petals of crimson and orange, and it was no effort to admire them as she crossed the Chinese rug. 'They're beautiful!'

'Miss Redding has a standing order with a firm of florists in Hamilton,' responded Sophie dampeningly. She opened another door to display an adjoining bedroom. 'Your bathroom is through there.'

'It's very nice. Thank you.'

Jaime refused to be daunted, and after another encompassing look about the room Sophie made for the door. 'Miss Redding will advise you of the eating arrangements tomorrow morning at breakfast,' she added brusquely. 'I'll have Samuel fetch your supper in fifteen minutes.'

Jaime was inclined to say that she didn't want any supper, thank you, but it would have seemed ungrateful to refuse. Besides, although she was tired, she was doubtful if she'd be able to sleep right away. She was far too excited to relax.

'My suitcase…' she ventured instead as Sophie went out the door, and the housekeeper turned back to give her a disdainful look.

'You'll find your suitcase in the bedroom,' she advised crisply. 'Samuel attended to it earlier. Even if Miss Redding hadn't decided to employ you, naturally you'd have been offered a bed for the night.'

'Oh.' Jaime felt suitably chastened. 'Thank you.'

'Miss Redding's orders,' declared Sophie, disclaiming all responsibility. 'Goodnight, Miss Harris. I hope you sleep well.'

Do you?

Jaime closed the door behind the housekeeper with a sense of relief. There was no doubt in her mind that Sophie didn't hope any such thing. Biting her lip, she turned the key before turning to reappraise her surroundings. Whatever else might happen, she was certainly going to have no complaints about her comfort while she was here.

It was almost dark, the twilight much shorter here than in England. The lamps Sophie had turned on had made the room clearly visible from outside, but before she drew the blinds she took a moment to admire the view.

There was a balcony beyond the windows, with a glass-topped table and a pair of rattan chairs. But it was the sweeping curve of the bay beyond the shrubbery that caught her imagination. And a sea which at this hour of the evening was painted with gold.

The room was even cosier when the curtains were drawn. A pair of rose-patterned sofas faced one another across a marble hearth, with the long low table that held the exotic flower arrangement between. There were several polished cabinets, one of which contained a television, and a single-stemmed mahogany table, and several matching mahogany chairs with velvet seats.

A huge Chinese rug covered most of the floor, but in the bedroom next door a cream shag pile was soft beneath her feet. Kicking off her shoes, she allowed her toes to curl into the carpet, imagining how disappointed her predecessor must have felt to be leaving all this behind.

The bedroom was dominated by a large, colonial-style bed, whose ruched counterpane matched the ruched silk curtains at the bedroom windows. The colour scheme of cream and gold was echoed in pale striped wallpaper, with the dark mahogany armoire and chest of drawers proving an attractive contrast.

Her suitcase was waiting on the padded ottoman at the foot of the bed, and she was releasing the clasps when she heard someone knock at the outer door. Her supper, she guessed ruefully, going to answer it. Whatever faults Sophie had, efficiency wasn't one of them.

The tall, ebony-skinned man who had brought her tray was probably Sophie's husband, she decided, though, unlike the housekeeper, he was inclined to be friendly. Setting the tray on the circular table, he took a little time to tell her what was under the silver lids, and then wished her a good night before he left.

Closing the door after him, Jaime leaned back against it, feeling a little less alien after his visit. It wasn't her fault, after all, that Kristin Spencer had been dismissed.

She was just grateful for the opportunity it had given her.

After unpacking her suitcase and exploring the sensuous luxury of the bathroom, Jaime sat down to her meal with some reluctance. She really wasn't hungry, but conversely she was too hyped up to go to bed, and the spicy shrimps with sauce were quite delicious. She left the medallions of veal, and nibbled on the strawberry shortcake, even if it wasn't particularly wise to eat something so sweet before going to bed. But, she told herself, she needed the sugar to maintain her optimism, and she'd never tasted such a delicious dessert before.

A small bottle of wine had accompanied the meal, and before going for her shower Jaime emptied the bottle into her glass, and stepped out onto the balcony. The shifting waters of the bay were no longer visible, but they were still audible, and she propped her hip against the rail and breathed deeply of the soft, salt-laden air. She was here, she thought incredulously. She was going to work with Catriona Redding. 'Forgive me, Dad,' she whispered, 'but I had to see what she was like for myself.'

CHAPTER TWO

DOMINIC awakened with a foul taste in his mouth. And a headache, he discovered, when he lifted his head off the pillow. Which wasn't so surprising, really. He'd drunk the better part of a bottle of Scotch the night before.

But it was the reason why he'd drunk the Scotch that made him want to bury his head in the pillow again and drag the sheet, which was all that was covering him, over his head. Catriona, damn her, was making his life difficult, and he sometimes actually found himself wishing his father had never married her.

Or died so soon, he appended ruefully, leaving him in such an invidious position. He thrust the sheet aside, and propped himself up on his elbows. If Lawrence Redding had still been alive, his life would have been so much simpler.

Sliding his long legs out of bed, he got rather unsteadily to his feet. The room rocked for a moment, but then steadied, and, promising himself he wouldn't let this happen again, Dominic trudged across the carpeted floor.

Through the slatted blinds, the sun was just beginning to gild the arched roofs of the cabanas that flanked the pool. The lushness of the gardens gave the place a tropical appearance at this time of the year, and he couldn't deny that he still regarded this place as home.

Beyond the pool and the gardens, dunes sloped away towards a stretch of white sand. The curve of Copperhead Bay formed an almost perfect backdrop, the ocean creaming softly on the shore. The tide was going out, leaving a tracery of rock pools that reflected the strengthening rays of the rising sun. His father had built this house to take full advantage of the view, and Dominic never tired of its timeless beauty.

Had never thought there might come a time when he would be forced to make a choice, he reflected wearily. After all, when his father married Catriona, he had been only sixteen. He'd never dreamt that in less than twenty years Lawrence Redding would be dead.

He was pondering the beneficial effects of an early morning dip when he saw someone appear from around the side of the house. A woman, he saw at once—a tall woman, dressed in trousers and a shirt, with a thick plait of rust-coloured hair draped over one shoulder. She had her arms wrapped about her body as she walked, and she acted as if she wasn't really aware of where she was.

He sighed. He knew who she must be, of course. She was his stepmother's new assistant, who'd apparently arrived from England the day before. Catriona had omitted to tell him that she had had a London employment agency find her another assistant. Just as she had omitted to tell him that while he was in New York she'd dismissed Kristin Spencer.

Poor Kristin. His lips twisted. He should have warned her that Catriona didn't like competition. And judging from his first impression of the woman by the pool she had gone for experience over beauty this time.

He grimaced, not liking the cynicism that was creeping into his consciousness these days. Catriona's fault, of course, but it was his own fault too for allowing himself to be influenced by her. Perhaps, if he'd had more success in his marriage than his father had, he'd have overcome the tendency. As it was, it was far too easy to accept his stepmother's interpretation of events, and if he wasn't careful he'd become just like her, taking what he wanted from life, without considering the consequences.

He frowned. He wondered what had attracted this woman to leave an apparently successful career in London to come and work in Bermuda. He supposed the idea was glamorous enough, but after a few weeks in the islands would she, like Kristin, be eager for some kind of diversion? After all, this estate was a good twelve miles from Hamilton, and apart from the obvious attractions of swimming and sunbathing there wasn't a lot to do. Even the islanders themselves spent regular breaks in the United Kingdom or the United States, and Dominic knew he'd go stir crazy himself if he was obliged to live here all year round.

Catriona had said this woman was a fan, that she'd left the lucrative position she'd enjoyed at the university to work with a writer she admired, but Dominic found that hard to believe. Or was that just another example of his cynicism? he wondered wryly. There was no doubt that his father's publishing house had benefited greatly from Catriona's novels.

Shaking his head, he forced himself to leave the woman to her solitary walk and went into the adjoining bathroom. A cool shower achieved what the ocean had denied him, and after towelling himself dry he ran an exploratory hand over his roughening jawline. He needed a shave, but he couldn't be bothered to attend to that right now. Instead, ignoring the warnings of his conscience, he pulled on a pair of frayed, knee-length denims and a black vest, and left his rooms.

The house was cool and quiet. Despite her sometimes strict working schedule, his stepmother rarely stirred before 8 a.m. Unlike himself, she was one of those people who could sleep whatever the circumstances, emerging from her room each morning with that fresh, unblemished appearance he knew so well.

Whatever else Catriona possessed, she was not troubled by a conscience—unlike himself.

Like many of the homes in Bermuda, the house was

two-storeyed, with a hipped roof, and a huge under-ground storage tank for rain water. It was always a source of interest to tourists that despite the lushness of its vegetation Bermuda had no actual water supply. But happily the islands were blessed with sufficient rain to fill the tanks, and Dominic had never tasted purer water in his life.

Descending the curving staircase into the Italian-tiled hall, Dominic paused for a moment to lace his canvas deck shoes. Here, evidence of his father's interest in sculpture was present in the marble likeness of an eight-eenth-century nude that stood beside the archway into a cream- and rose-painted drawing room, while a pair of Venetian sconces provided light on the rare occasions when the power supply was interrupted.

Because he was so familiar with the house, Dominic paid little attention to the elegance of his surroundings. His father had built the house when he was little more than a schoolboy, and it was as familiar to him as his own apartment in Manhattan. Though perhaps not as comfortable these days, he conceded, with some irony.

Leaving the hall by means of the glass-panelled door that led into the sun-filled morning room, he crossed the braided carpet to reach the windows. Releasing the catch, he slid the patio door along, and stepped outside.

The warmth that met him was hypnotic. The coolness of the house was such a contrast to the sensuous heat of the morning and even there, in the shade of the terrace, his skin prickled in anticipation of the sun's assault. There was little humidity, and although it could get very hot in the middle of the day it was seldom unbearable. Right now, at the beginning of July, summer was at its height, and apart from a few fleecy clouds the sky above was clear.

Breathing deeply, he stepped out into the sunlight. From here, it was possible to see the whole of the pool area, and he was almost disappointed to find that the woman he'd seen earlier had disappeared. Not that he had any interest in her, he assured himself drily. He knew better than to show any partiality for Catriona's protégées. He was just curious to know what had really persuaded her to take this job.

He sighed, and glanced at the watch on his wrist. It was barely seven o'clock, and apart from having to speak to his office later the day was his own. A prospect that didn't please him as it should, he realised grimly, wishing he had not succumbed to Catriona's invitation to recuperate at Copperhead Bay. Dammit, he had only had a cold. Just because he had neglected it, and it had turned to pneumonia, that was no reason to leave New York at one of the busiest times of the year.

The trouble was, her invitation had come when his spirits were at their lowest ebb, and he'd given in without really considering what he was taking on. It was over a year since his father's death, and he should have known that Catriona would consider twelve months more than long enough to mourn her late husband.

A shadow moved at the far side of the pool. He'd been wrong, he realised at once. The woman hadn't disappeared. She'd been there all the time, hidden by the canopy of a striped lounge chair, but now she had got to her feet, and her consternation at seeing him was evident in every startled line of her body.

Dominic hesitated. It would be easy enough to turn and go back into the house, and save her the trouble of having to explain herself to him. But something, some latent spark of interest that he would otherwise have denied, kept him where he was. Made him move forward in fact, to intercept her automatic intention to escape.

'Good morning,' he said easily, shoving his hands into the back pockets of his cut-offs to avoid the necessity of a more formal introduction. 'It's a beautiful morning, isn't it?'

'Beautiful, yes,' she answered, with evident unwillingness. And then, because she obviously thought she'd been trespassing, she added, 'I'm sorry if I disturbed you.'

'You didn't,' he assured her, although she had, inadvertently at least. There was something about her that stirred a vague sense of recognition inside him, and although he had not been wrong about her age her pale features were not unappealing. 'Miss—Harrison, isn't it?'

'Harris,' she corrected him at once, one hand reaching to circle her throat. 'Um—Jaime Harris,' she appended, the unbuttoned sleeve of her shirt falling back to reveal the vulnerable curve of her elbow. 'Mr—er—'

He was curiously reluctant to tell her. 'Redding,' he supplied briefly. 'Dominic Redding. Catriona's—stepson.'

'Oh!' Was it his imagination or did that information cause a little of the tenseness to leave her face? 'How do you do?'

So formal!

His lips curled. 'Reasonably well, mostly,' he replied, with a wry smile. 'How about you?'

'Oh—I—yes. I'm fine,' she stammered, her tongue appearing to moisten her lips, and Dominic was surprised to find himself studying her features with rather more discrimination.

His first impression had not been entirely wrong, he decided. She was older than Kristin had been, and decidedly more reserved in her approach to men. But there was some merit in those wide-set grey eyes, which avoided his gaze more often than they met it, and her mouth, for all its nervousness, had a surprisingly sensual lower lip.

All in all, she was not what he had expected, Dominic mused, half wishing he hadn't effected the introduction. Catriona wouldn't approve of his socialising with the paid help, and for all he seldom obeyed her dictates he didn't want to make life any more difficult than it already was.

'Do you live here, Mr Redding?'

While he had been brooding over past mistakes, she had evidently gained in confidence. Her question caught him unawares, and although he guessed it was innocent enough he objected to being interrogated.

'Sometimes,' he answered obliquely, and he could almost sense the way she took in his reply, and stored it away for future reference. He had been right, he thought again. She was nothing like Kristin. He wasn't altogether sure he trusted her.

'Sometimes?' she echoed now, in that diffident way she had of speaking. 'It's not your home, then?'

'It was my father's house. I live in New York,' declared Dominic, not quite knowing why he suddenly felt so defensive. He turned the tables. 'Tell me, Miss Harris, why would someone with a degree in English, and an obviously secure job in a London university, give it all up to come and work as Catriona's secretary?'

That seemed to baulk her. But only briefly.

'Why—I'm a great fan of your stepmother's!' she exclaimed, with rather more spirit than she had shown thus far. 'It was a wonderful opportunity.'

Was it?

Dominic's mouth drew in. Her enthusiasm seemed genuine enough, and yet there was something about the way she'd said the words that made him doubt her sincerity. But what other reason could she have for coming to the island? Why was he looking for problems, when there were none to find?

'Well, I hope it lives up to your expectations,' he averred, deciding to curtail their conversation. She was here. Catriona had employed her—temporarily, at least. And he intended to return to New York in a few days anyway.

'Thank you.'

She seemed to sense his irritation, for after allowing him a polite look from beneath thick, gold-tipped lashes she moved towards the colonnade that led back to her apartment.

But, as he was reaching to pull his vest over his head, preparatory to taking a swim, her voice drifted back to him. 'Your father's dead?' she asked, and Dominic jerked the top down again, and turned to regard her with dark, angry eyes.

'I beg your pardon?'

'I'm sorry.' Her nervousness didn't seem feigned now. Quite the opposite. 'But you said—you said it *was* your father's house. Is Miss—*Mrs*—Redding a widow?'

Dominic's nostrils flared. 'That would seem a fair assumption,' he responded curtly. 'Why?'

'Oh—no reason.' A faint smile brushed across that sensual mouth. She gestured towards her rooms. 'I'd better go and get ready for breakfast.'

And get rid of those ugly trousers, thought Dominic grimly, tossing off his vest and reaching for the zip of his cut-offs. But then his hand stilled. Dammit, he wasn't wearing any swimming shorts. It wasn't that he was bashful. He was long past the age of feeling any callow modesty about his body; it was simply that he didn't care for the idea of her watching him. There was something about Miss Harris that disturbed his equilibrium.

His mood completely soured now, Dominic snatched up his top and strode back to the terrace. Slamming the patio door aside, he plunged into the house—and came face to face with his stepmother.

With his eyes still dazzled from the sunlight outside, Dominic was even less inclined to be tolerant. 'Dammit, Cat,' he muttered, pulling back from her reaching hands, 'what the hell are you doing up at this hour of the morning?'

His stepmother regarded him with cool indulgence. In

a coral-pink satin wrapper, she was slim and elegant, her make-up light, but faultless, despite the early hour.

'I heard voices, darling,' she defended herself silkily, her nails brushing softly against his skin. She viewed his half-naked appearance with evident enjoyment. 'Was Sophie on the prowl again?'

'No.' Dominic bit off the word, wishing he didn't have to explain who he'd been talking to. But Catriona wouldn't be satisfied until she had the story from him, and it was obviously more sensible to be honest from the start. 'I met your new secretary.'

'Miss Harris?' Catriona's delicately tinted lips tightened, and Dominic prepared himself for the remonstrance that he was sure was to come. 'What did you think of her, darling? Quite a change from Kristin, isn't she? And such a frump! Is that what universities are turning out these days?'

He knew a quite absurd desire to defend the woman, but he suppressed the urge. So long as Catriona thought she was unthreatening, Miss Harris's job was safe. Besides, it was only what he had thought, seeing her from the window. His later opinion had been influenced by a ridiculous awareness of her sexuality.

'Who knows?' he responded, grateful for the diversion. 'She seems to admire your work, as you said.'

'Mmm.' Catriona absorbed the compliment indifferently, her attention focused now on his mouth. Her tongue circled her lips. 'Kiss me good morning, darling. Then I'll ask Sophie to serve us breakfast on the terrace. It's not often we get the chance to be alone at this time of day.'

Dominic bent and brushed her mouth with his own, but when he would have drawn back again her slim arms circled his neck. 'More,' she whispered huskily, her small teeth nibbling at his ear. 'I've got a better idea. Why don't we have breakfast in bed?'

Dominic's hands on her shoulders propelled her away

from him. 'Not this morning, Cat,' he told her flatly, even though the blood was racing through his veins. He'd wanted her for ever, it seemed; ever since his father had first brought her to this house. But he couldn't despoil his father's memory by making her his mistress. Not yet, at any rate.

'Why not?' Catriona looked sulky now, her thin lips drawn down in a frustrated curve. 'When are you going to accept that we've waited long enough? Dom, Larry has been dead for more than a year!'

'I know.'

Dominic lifted his vest and tugged it over his head, using the action to avoid her resentful eyes. Dammit, he knew better than anyone how long it was since they had buried his father, and of how mixed his feelings had been because Lawrence Redding was gone.

'If you're not careful, I shall begin to think you don't love me anymore,' Catriona accused him now, her eyes sparkling with more anger than grief. 'I thought when you agreed to come here to recuperate that you'd realised we can't go on like this any longer. I need you, Dom. I want to be with you. And I always thought that was what you wanted, too.'

'It is!'

Dominic's jaw compressed, and the urge to ignore his scruples and take her in his arms almost overcame his common sense. But for all he was desperate to make love to her this wasn't the time. He owed his father much more than a lousy twelve months' grace.

'Then why—?'

'Look, we'll have breakfast together, right?' he interrupted her tersely. 'It's too early in the day to have a conversation like this. I'll speak to Sophie while you go and put some clothes on. Besides, didn't you tell me you'd be having breakfast with your new assistant? You can't let her down.'

'But you can let me down, it seems,' retorted Catriona

coldly, tightening the cord of her robe about her slim
waist. 'You're a cruel bastard, Dom. Sometimes I wonder why I care about you so much.'

Dominic sighed. 'Cat—'

'Don't say anything more.' Catriona held up a quell-
ing hand, and walked haughtily towards the door. 'And
don't bother joining us for breakfast. As you say, my
work—or in this case my assistant—must come first.'

Dominic grimaced as she disappeared, but although
he was sure he would pay for it later he didn't regret
having made a stand. During the past twelve months, his
relationship with Catriona had developed faster than
even he could have imagined, and he knew it was time
to slow it down.

It was strange—he could remember the first time he'd
seen Catriona as if it were yesterday. He'd been fifteen
years old at the time, home from school in Boston,
spending his summer swimming and sailing, and loafing
around the house.

He'd been used to being on his own in those days.
His mother had been killed in a freak skiing accident
when he was only six, and his father had coped with his
grief by burying himself in his work. The publishing
house in New York, which Dominic's grandfather had
founded, had kept him busy, and Lawrence Redding had
never really learned how to delegate.

Catriona—Markham, as she was known then—had
been a young author from England. She'd written a couple of rather poor detective novels that hadn't found a
publisher, and her agent had sent her latest manuscript
to Goldman and Redding in New York in the hope of
appealing to the lucrative American market.

Dominic didn't know if his father had considered that
first manuscript might be worthy of publication, or
whether, on meeting her, he'd just been blinded by the
woman's beauty. In any event, six months later she'd
become Mrs Lawrence Redding, and six months after

that her first romantic historical novel had been published under the name of Catriona Redding.

He knew it had been his father's influence which had first made her books so successful. With the promotion he'd given that first book and Catriona's own personality sparkling on every talk-show nationwide, it would have been hard to fail. Dominic knew from his own experience that it wasn't always the book itself that put it on the best-seller lists. But it had been the second and all the subsequent successes that had made Catriona Redding a household name. In writing romantic historicals she had found her niche, and each new title had attracted more and more readers.

It would have been ungracious not to admit that Goldman and Redding had benefited greatly from the alliance, but, as Catriona frequently said when she was interviewed, she owed her success to Larry for pointing her in the right direction. And, although towards the end of her husband's life Catriona had often spoken of the possible advantages of writing for a larger publishing house, she had never actually deserted her husband's firm.

His own reaction to acquiring a new stepmother was not something Dominic was particularly proud of. He'd always thought she was too young for his father, and, at sixteen, he'd just been beginning to explore his own sexuality. He could—and had—defended his attraction to her by pointing out her own culpability. For all she'd remained faithful to his father, she had done nothing to diffuse his fascination.

Indeed, he'd sometimes wondered what she would have done if he'd had less respect for his father. There was no doubt that she'd enjoyed flirting with him, and she'd begun to regard him as a permanent fixture in her life. Although she was about ten years older than he was, she'd always behaved as if they had more in common than she and his father, and only when Lawrence was present had she behaved as a stepmother should.

It had been easier when he'd gone away to college. Away from Catriona's influence, he'd begun to notice other women, and when he was twenty-two he'd married the sister of one of his college friends. Mary Beth was sweet and gentle, everything Catriona was not, and although his parents had attended the wedding Catriona had soon made it plain that his wife was not welcome at Copperhead Bay.

She hadn't said it in so many words, of course. It was still his father's house, and Lawrence Redding had taken quite a shine to his new daughter-in-law. But Catriona had disliked Mary Beth on sight, and had lost no opportunity to belittle her. Or to show her hostility, Dominic conceded grimly, so that even Mary Beth was made aware of it, and had refused to go where she wasn't wanted.

It had made things impossible for him—as it had been intended to do—but instead of blaming Catriona Dominic had blamed his wife. He'd convinced himself that she must have done something to offend his stepmother, and Mary Beth had eventually forced him to choose between his family and herself.

It had been no contest, he mused now, half-bitterly. His infatuation for his stepmother had been too strong, and Catriona, damn her, had known that from the start. Apart from anything else, she'd banked on the fact that he'd do nothing to hurt his father—even if he had drawn the line at being involved in the production of his stepmother's books.

His father's sudden death of a heart attack at the age of sixty-four had changed a lot of things. Not least the fact that Catriona was now free to do whatever she liked. Less than three months after his father's funeral, she had let Dominic know that she knew how he had always felt about her, and that there was no reason now for her to deny the fact that she reciprocated his feelings. She'd said she'd always known that her marriage to Lawrence Redding had been a mistake, but that luckily she still had plenty of time to make amends.

But that had been too much, even for Dominic. Coming close on the heels of the unwelcome news that his father had expected him to take over as nominal head of Goldman and Redding, he had felt stifled. He had never wanted to work for his father's firm, and although his feelings for Catriona hadn't lessened they had altered. He still wanted her; of course he did. But he had no intention of abusing his father's memory by bedding his widow almost before he was cold in his grave.

But the fact remained that, although Catriona had inherited the house on Bermuda, where she'd written all her best-sellers, and the bulk of his father's personal fortune, Lawrence Redding had left the publishing company to his son. And although Dominic had trained as a lawyer, not an editor, and had been working for a successful firm of attorneys in Boston at the time of his father's death, he'd felt obliged to resign his position and move to New York.

Which was probably the biggest mistake he'd ever made, he conceded now, pushing his hands back into his pockets and staring broodingly over the pool. With Catriona as his client—as well as his would-be lover—he was struggling. He knew as well as anyone that if he offended Catriona, and she found an alternative publisher, Goldman and Redding would suffer.

But what else could he have done, given the terms of his father's last will and testament? Lawrence Redding had wanted him to take over the running of the company; he'd wanted him to produce Catriona's books in his place. God, hadn't he ever suspected how Dominic felt about her? Or was this his way of showing that the two of them had his blessing?

Dominic scowled. There really was no reason for him

to continue resisting the inevitable. Catriona was right; it was over a year since his father's death. There was nothing—and no one—to prevent him from making them both happy. So why didn't he go upstairs now and finish what he'd started a few minutes ago?

But still he stayed there, and presently a pair of curiously knowing grey eyes drifted across his inner vision. He wondered how Catriona's solemn-faced secretary would react if she knew what he was thinking. Would she get some vicarious thrill from picturing them together, or would she be disgusted by the overtones of incest inherent in the relationship?

The latter, he suspected brusquely, the urge to go and give Catriona what she wanted rapidly fading. The moment when he might have given in was past, and his mood had darkened. Deciding to forgo breakfast, he pushed the door open again and left the building. In this frame of mind, he was better on his own.

CHAPTER THREE

'Do you drive?'

Jaime looked up with a start. Something, some sixth sense perhaps, had warned her she was no longer alone, and she slipped the earphones down around her neck. She had spent the afternoon transcribing the tape of letters Catriona Redding had recorded that morning, and she blamed the fact that she was tired for the disturbing ripple of awareness that spread along her veins at that moment.

Dominic Redding was propped in the doorway of the small office that adjoined Catriona's study, his hip lodged against one side of the frame, his hand braced against the other. He looked as if he'd been working out: his cotton shorts were clinging to the powerful muscles of his thighs and his grey vest was soaked with sweat. She could smell the heat of his body, even though there were several feet between them. It was not an unpleasant scent, but the knowledge of what she was thinking brought an unwilling trace of colour to her cheeks.

'Um—what did you—?'

She hadn't seen him since the previous morning, when he'd come upon her so unexpectedly beside the pool, and she'd begun to think he must have left the island. He'd told her he lived in New York, after all, and surely he couldn't have much in common with his stepmother.

'I asked if you could drive,' he repeated, at her stammering response, and Jaime knew her prevarication had been necessary. She wasn't used to being disconcerted by a man, and this man put the kind of thoughts into her head that she hadn't had since she was a teenager. For

33

heaven's sake, she chided herself, irritated by this evidence of what she regarded as her own immaturity. She'd been holding her own in the male-dominated world of the university since she was eighteen. What on earth was wrong with her now?

Dominic Redding was speaking again, and she forced herself to concentrate on what he was saying. 'Catriona seldom uses a car herself, and I thought you might be interested in seeing a little more of the island. It's Saturday tomorrow, so I guess it's your day off.'

'Yes.'

'Yes, what?' His dark eyes were unerringly intent. 'Yes, you can drive, or yes, you'd like to see more of the island? There's a twenty miles an hour speed limit in operation if you're nervous.'

'I'm not nervous.' Jaime was used to driving her father about London, but she didn't want to go into that. 'And yes, I can drive. I've been driving for—well, for years.'

'Great.' A lock of damp dark hair flopped onto his forehead and he thrust it back with an impatient hand. 'So—how does the idea grab you? I believe the shops in Hamilton are pretty good.'

Jaime let her hands rest on the keys of the word processor, taking care not to put any weight on them. It was kind of him to think of her, she thought, trying to get his suggestion in perspective. Two days of working for Catriona had persuaded her that she would be unlikely to think of such a thing. Catriona was, quite simply, the most self-motivated person she had ever met.

'I—it sounds good,' she answered at last. 'But I'm not sure if Miss Redding will expect me to work.'

'Well, okay.' He shrugged. 'Let me know if you decide to take me up on it. There's an open-topped four-by-four that's seldom used.'

'Thank you.'

Jaime was grateful—and for the interruption, too. She

had been typing almost solidly for the past couple of hours, and for someone who was more used to grading essays the consistent glare of the computer screen was tiring. Her eyes were probably red-rimmed with exhaustion, she thought gloomily, wondering what Dominic Redding must think of her. Not that it mattered, she assured herself with feeling. He was not the kind of man who attracted her.

'You're welcome.'

His drawling response was vaguely ironic, but she hardly had time to evaluate his humour before the door to Catriona Redding's study was jerked open. 'For heaven's sake, Miss Harris,' she was exhorting as she stormed into her secretary's room, 'must I remind you that I'm trying to work in——? Oh!' This as she saw who Jaime had been talking to. Her tone changed to one of guarded approval. 'Dominic!' She moistened her lips. 'Were you looking for me?'

'Oh, I think I'd know where to find you,' he replied, with a strangely mocking expression on his face. 'No. As a matter of fact, I came to see your secretary. I've offered her the use of the Toyota.'

Catriona's mouth tightened. 'Have you really?' she remarked, linking her long fingers together at her waist. 'I don't recall you asking my permission.'

Dominic's eyes narrowed. 'I didn't think it was necessary.'

'No?'

'No.' His jaw compressed. 'The vehicle never leaves the garage, for God's sake!'

'Nevertheless——'

'Nevertheless, it's yours, is that it?' Dominic countered angrily, straightening his spine against the jamb. 'Well, okay. Forget the car. I'll take her myself. I assume the Harley-Davidson is still mine?'

Catriona's face crumpled. 'That won't be necessary,' she said, and now Jaime was amazed to see what looked like tears sparkling at the corners of her vivid blue eyes. 'If—if I don't need it, of course she can use the Toyota. I was just being bitchy. I'm sorry. I've been half out of my mind since you took off.'

Dominic looked impatient now, and Jaime wondered why his stepmother's mood swings should cause such acrimony between them. Catriona was like a child, she thought incredulously—perverse and malicious one minute, appealingly tearful the next. She acted as if her stepson's good opinion was all that mattered to her, and Jaime knew a sudden sense of unease that had nothing to do with her own position in the household.

And, as if realising that she was an unwilling spectator to their confrontation, Dominic pulled a wry face. 'Hey, I need a shower,' he said, including both women in his sweeping gaze. Then, addressing himself to Catriona, he added, 'We'll finish this discussion later. Ask Sophie to send me up a couple of beers, will you?'

'I've got some beer in my fridge!' exclaimed Catriona at once, gesturing at the room behind her. 'And I'm— dying to hear what you've been doing. Samuel said he thought you'd gone to the marina—'

'Later,' said Dominic, once again including Jaime in his response. 'You don't want me to catch another chill, do you? This air-conditioning's fixing to freeze my—' he grimaced '—toes!'

Short of causing another unpleasant scene, there was little more Catriona could say, and with a rueful nod in Jaime's direction Dominic disappeared out of the door. Leaving a distinctly chilly atmosphere behind him, thought Jaime unhappily. An atmosphere that had nothing to do with the air-conditioning at all.

Alone with her employer, Jaime fixed her gaze on the computer screen that only moments before she had been grateful to avoid. But somehow she had the feeling that anything she said might precipitate an argument, and that, far from backing down, in this case the woman would enjoy the opportunity to make someone else look small.

'Have you finished yet?' she asked at last, and Jaime had no choice but to make eye contact with her.

'I've finished typing your notes,' she replied pleasantly. She touched the Dictaphone. 'But I'm not sure how many letters are left on the tape.'

Catriona took a deep breath. 'Do you find it interesting?' she asked. 'The manuscript, I mean.' The previous day they had spent organising a working schedule, and this was the first opportunity Jaime had had to transcribe the handwritten pages. 'My previous secretary used to give me her opinion.' Her lips twisted. 'Poor Kristin; she didn't have a clue.'

Jaime swallowed. 'I think it's very interesting,' she said, not falling into that trap. If Catriona was looking for a fight, she could look somewhere else. She had no intention of jeopardising her position by attempting to guess what her employer wanted to hear.

Catriona seemed to grow impatient, and brushed a scarlet nail across Jaime's knuckles where they rested on the keys. 'So tactful,' she said. 'So efficient, too.' She paused, and the younger woman knew an almost overwhelming impulse to move away from her. 'I hope you're not going to prove too good to be true.'

Jaime caught her lower lip between her teeth, and bit down hard. The pain steadied her. 'I hope not,' she managed politely, resisting the urge to replace her headphones and end this conversation once and for all. 'Would you like me to print the pages I've already typed?'

'That won't be necessary.' Catriona's tone hardened. 'No, I suggest you print them and check them yourself before passing them on to me. I shall expect a faultless copy when you've finished. Let's hope you have no more distractions, shall we?'

Jaime caught her breath, sensing they were coming to

the crux of what Catriona really wanted to say. She
wasn't hanging about here just to annoy her secretary.
She wanted to explain what had happened earlier—to
justify her own behaviour, so that Jaime wouldn't get
the wrong idea.

'Um—Mr Redding only stopped off in passing,' she
said, and then wished she hadn't when Catriona impaled
her with an accusatory gaze.

'In passing?' she echoed. 'Do you know where
Dominic has been?'

'Of course not.' Jaime now found herself in exactly
the position she'd hoped to avoid. 'I just meant—he was
only here for a few minutes.'

'I know exactly how long he was here,' retorted
Catriona coldly. 'I know precisely the moment when you
stopped typing and started flirting with him.'

Jaime gasped then. She couldn't help it. 'I—I wasn't
flirting with him,' she protested, even though her scarlet
cheeks probably proclaimed just the opposite. 'He—he
asked me if I could drive. That was all.'

'Really?' Catriona regarded her between narrowed
lids. 'Well, if you didn't flirt with Dom, you must be
the first woman he's met who hasn't done so,' she declared contemptuously.

Jaime lifted her shoulders. 'I'm sorry.'

'Oh, don't be sorry.' Catriona was impatient now, as
if regretting her earlier outburst. 'But he is a dangerously
attractive man, don't you think? Or do your tastes lie in
another direction?'

Jaime stared at her. 'I beg your pardon?'

'Well, you are—what was it you put in your application?—twenty-eight?'

'Twenty-nine.'

'You see—' Catriona spread her hands '—and you've
never been married. Surely I can be forgiven for being
curious?'

Jaime wanted to knock the smug expression off

Catriona's face, but she knew better than to show her hand that way. Instead, she sat there like some stiffly postured dummy, letting Catriona walk all over her.

She doesn't know me, she kept telling herself; she doesn't know who I am. If she did, it would be different. To her, I'm just another female, who might, or might not, become a nuisance so far as Dominic is concerned. Catriona is just laying out the ground rules; making sure her new secretary doesn't get the wrong idea.

'It's not important,' she said now, managing to sound as if it really wasn't. 'You needn't worry, Mrs Redding. Your stepson is in no danger from me.'

'*Miss* Redding,' said Catriona irritably. 'It's *Miss* Redding. Please don't forget. And I never think of Dominic as my stepson. He's a man, and I'm a woman.' Her lips softened. 'Do you understand?'

Jaime felt suddenly sick. She could feel the colour draining out of her face now, and she prayed Catriona wouldn't notice it, too. Dear God, what was she saying? That she and Dominic Redding were lovers? Jaime couldn't believe it. It wasn't possible. She had to be twenty years older than he was, at least.

'Have I shocked you?'

To her horror, Jaime realised that Catriona was actually enjoying this. Now that she'd betrayed her sordid little secret, she seemed to be hoping that Jaime wouldn't let her down. Catriona wanted her to show some reaction, preferably admiration. After all, Dominic Redding was a very attractive man. Jaime was not unaware of that.

'I—it's nothing to do with me,' she muttered, wishing the woman would just go away and leave her alone. She'd had enough of feeling like a mouse in the paws of a rather vicious she-cat. In all her feeble calculations, she'd never allowed for this.

'But it is to do with you,' Catriona persisted, though to Jaime's relief she moved towards the open door of her study. 'After all, you're a member of the household now. I want you to understand why I was so upset earlier.'

In a pig's eye!

For all the chaotic state of her emotions, Jaime still knew a lie when she heard one. Catriona didn't care what she thought of her. She just wanted to warn her that if she had any ideas about Dominic she should forget them—or take the consequences.

Like Kristin? Which might explain Sophie's attitude, as well.

Schooling her features to an impassive blandness, Jaime chose the least provocative path she knew. 'Will you be wanting to examine these pages tonight, *Miss* Redding?' she enquired politely. 'I should think I could have them checked in about an hour.'

The implications of what she had learned that afternoon struck Jaime more strongly that evening.

After Samuel had delivered her supper tray, as usual, she carried it out onto the balcony, and seated herself in one of the cushioned rattan chairs. Yesterday morning, Catriona had informed her that although they might sometimes have breakfast or lunch together she would be expected to dine in her own quarters. It was nothing less than Jaime had anticipated. She'd read enough books to know how live-in employees were usually treated.

Tonight, however, she could not maintain the spirit of objectivity that had carried her through the two days since her arrival. Restlessness, and the undoubted shock she had received when Catriona had spoken of her relationship with Dominic, had left her in a state of raw ambivalence. She no longer knew whether what she was doing was entirely sensible; she didn't even know if she wanted to stay.

It had all seemed so simple in London.

Her father's death, and the discovery of the newspaper clippings, had shed a whole new light on her own identity, and, although in the beginning she'd never had any intention of doing anything about it, seeing Catriona's advertisement as she had had given her this crazy idea of applying for the job.

After all, she'd thought, if she could arrange it, what did she have to lose? She had no family ties to worry about, and it wasn't as if it was going to be a permanent arrangement. All she'd needed was a couple of weeks' leave-of-absence, and with the long summer vacation in the offing that hadn't been a problem.

And, when she'd applied for the job, she hadn't really believed that she might be appointed. After all, it was some years since she'd done any secretarial work, even if she used a computer to store her notes. There were so many competent secretaries in the market-place, but she was called for a second interview, and ultimately told that, subject to Catriona's approval, the job was hers.

So where was the excitement now that she had felt then? Why had everything suddenly gone so flat? She knew the answer, of course—had known it from the moment Catriona had first walked into her study When she'd regarded Janne with that cold, assessing smile, she'd suspected then she'd made a huge mistake.

But then she'd determined to overcome her apprehension. She'd put her misgivings down to the way she was feeling, but now she was not so sure. She was beginning to wonder if the doubts she had had might not have been a warning. And she'd ignored it because the idea of flying over three thousand miles, just to turn around and fly back again, had seemed childish and immature.

She sighed. What had happened, after all, to cause all this soul-searching? Was it just because she'd found out Catriona was having an affair? For heaven's sake, the woman's sexual habits had nothing to do with why she had come here. It was natural that she should have a man in her life. She was a beautiful woman. So why not?

The truth was a much more personal thing than she wanted to acknowledge. Although she barely knew Dominic Redding—and had certainly no expectation that he might ever find her attractive—the idea that he might be having an affair with his father's widow overstepped the bounds of decency, so far as Jaime was concerned.

Perhaps she was a prude; perhaps her opinion was hopelessly provincial. The world of the university did tend to insulate one from the more sordid side of life. Why should it matter to her what Catriona and her step-son did in the privacy of their own apartments? Wasn't she judging them unfairly, without knowing any of the facts?

Whatever, the news had cast an uneasy shadow over the situation. She had had such high hopes when she'd come here, yet slowly but surely they were all being eaten away. But what had she expected from a woman who, twenty-seven years ago, had abandoned her husband and baby? She should have let Cathryn Michaels stay dead. Resurrecting icons was always a risky business...

CHAPTER FOUR

DOMINIC allowed the wave to carry him all the way in to the shore, and then pushed himself to his feet and walked up out of the ocean. Water streamed over his shoulders from the overly long hair that lapped at his nape, and he raised a careless hand to push back the heavy dark strands. He'd have to get it cut before he went back to the office, he reflected, and scowled as the connotations of that thought soured his mood.

Picking up the towel he had dropped on the beach, he dried himself vigorously, warming his cooling flesh. Although the ocean was several degrees warmer here than it was off the coast of New York state, at this hour of the morning it could still feel chilly. But the exhilaration of the experience always made him feel good.

Or it did usually, he amended, drying his thighs, and then reaching for his jeans. This morning, he'd used the excuse of going for a swim to avoid having to make a decision about when he was leaving. After last night, he knew he couldn't put it off much longer.

Catriona had been particularly irritating the previous evening. Far from trying to understand his position, she had accused him of avoiding her, of avoiding any discussion about their future. She'd even asked if he found her new assistant attractive, as if that were relevant. He grimaced. She surely couldn't imagine he was interested in Jaime Harris. For God's sake, he'd been civil to the woman, that was all. Catriona's constant carping about his treatment of other females simply wasn't warranted.

He zipped up his jeans, leaving the button at his waist unfastened as he towelled his hair. Dammit, what kind of a life were they going to have together if she didn't trust him? Since his divorce from Mary Beth, he'd never had another serious relationship.

He looped the towel about his neck, and stared brooding-ingly towards the headland. Obviously the bug that had sapped his strength and brought him here was still infecting his system. Right now, he couldn't think about the future with any enthusiasm at all. God, he didn't even know what the future held, and the more Catriona pushed him, the more reluctant he was to placate her.

A shadow moved suddenly near the dunes that sloped down to the beach, and he stiffened. Dammit, he realised impatiently, it was that woman again: Jaime Harris. Had Catriona set her to spy on him as well?

The unlikelihood of that scenario brought a cynical compression to his lips. Catriona would never do that. Particularly not when the woman was younger than she was. More likely, she was still having a problem with sleeping. He knew what it was like to wake early in the morning and not be able to fall asleep again. He pulled a wry face. His being here at this hour was proof of that.

It was obvious from the way she was trying to melt back into the shadows that she was as unwilling to acknowledge the encounter as before. And he was tempted to let her go, without embarrassing her again. But what the hell? he thought. Maybe this was what he needed. Perhaps talking to someone else would lift the weight of his problems for a short while.

It couldn't have been much fun for her so far. Working for Catriona all day, and then being expected to entertain herself every evening, was not his idea of the ideal job. He'd noticed that, despite his invitation, she hadn't used the Toyota over the weekend. He suspected Catriona had kept her busy. When Catriona was in the throes of composition, she tended not to consider anyone's needs but her own.

Abandoning his mood of introspection, he turned and

looked directly at her, so that she was obliged either to acknowledge she had seen him or risk offending him by pretending she hadn't. A faint smile touched his lips as he watched her indecision, although he guessed the outcome was a foregone conclusion. He could almost sense what she was thinking, as she hovered between recognition and rejection, but he wasn't surprised when she gave in to his approach.

'Good morning,' he said as he sauntered, barefoot, across the sand towards her. His lips twitched. 'We must stop meeting like this.'

Her lips tightened. 'I'm sorry,' she said stiffly. 'I always seem to be invading your space.'

'It's a free country,' he responded carelessly, aware that her greeting had been less friendly than it might have been. Dammit, surely she wasn't offended because he'd accosted her? He couldn't believe she might be embarrassed by his half-naked state.

'You've been swimming,' she said, and it was more a statement than a question. She wanted to get away from him, he knew, but the courtesies had to be observed. Her formality amused him. It was such a refreshing change.

'Mmm,' he said, aware that he was studying her with rather more interest than he had done thus far. His first impressions of her had been too facile. There was intelligence, as well as perception, in her face.

And she had great legs, he noticed, his eyes dropping briefly below her waist. She'd found some shorts from somewhere, and the awful trousers had disappeared, revealing slender calves and neat ankles. Of course, they were not the sort of shorts he would have liked to see her wearing, he thought. With her waist, she didn't need to resort to an elasticated band, and they were cotton instead of silk. But he could imagine how she would look in the alternative, with a matching silk vest, instead of the baggy cotton T-shirt she had on.

'I was just going back,' she murmured, the faint flush of heat that stained her throat revealing she was not unaware of his appraisal.

For someone used to working with men, she was very sensitive, he reflected. He couldn't imagine any of the women of his acquaintance behaving that way. And she was a woman who had been prepared to leave her home and family, and take a job in completely alien surroundings, he appended as that beguiling trace of familiarity gripped him once again.

Dammit, did he know her? he wondered. Was that why she was regarding him as if he'd just crawled out from beneath the nearest stone? But no. Although he had been wary of her, she had shown no hostility towards him the first morning she was here, when he'd encountered her by the pool. On the contrary, it was he who had been suspicious of her motives. So what had happened since to cause her to change her mind? Catriona?

'You're not going for a swim?' he found himself saying now as she turned away, and her eyes darted disbelievingly to his face.

'A swim?'

'Why not?' he countered, not quite knowing why he had suggested it himself. Except that he wanted to dispel the animosity she seemed to be exhibiting towards him. For some crazy reason, he resented her regarding him as her enemy. Whatever Catriona had said—and he guessed it must be something to do with their relationship—this woman had no reason to censure him.

Her spine straightened, and she held up her head. 'I don't think so, Mr Redding.'

'You don't swim?'

'Of course I can swim.' Her voice was terse. 'But—I haven't brought a swimsuit with me.'

'To Bermuda?' His eyes mocked her.

'To the beach,' she amended curtly. 'And—unlike—unlike some people, I don't swim without one.'

'Unlike me, you mean?'

'I didn't say that, Mr Redding.'

'But you meant it.' He was actually beginning to enjoy himself. 'Haven't you ever been tempted to try it? I can assure you, it beats any of the alternatives.'

Her lips tightened. 'I'll take your word for it.'

'But you won't change your mind?'

She turned away. 'I have to go,' she said stiffly, and he realised she was using all her self-control to avoid saying something she might regret. After all, in her eyes he was her employer's—what? Stepson? Friend? *Lover?* Too close a relationship, certainly, to risk her job by calling his bluff.

'Must you?' he asked abruptly, and although she had put at least half a dozen steps between them she looked back.

'I—Mr Redding—'

'Call me Dominic,' he said easily, closing the space between them in a couple of strides. 'Look, I know you're not in a hurry, so why don't you keep me company? Walk with me along the beach, and I'll show you Spanish Cove.'

She took a deep breath. 'I don't think that would be entirely wise, do you?' she asked coolly.

'Wise?' His eyes narrowed. 'That's a curious word to use.'

'Is it?' She caught her lower lip between her teeth for a moment. 'I don't want to lose my job, Mr Redding.'

He frowned. 'Lose your job?' He shook his head. 'I'm not suggesting we spend the whole morning together. You'll be back in plenty of time to have breakfast with Catriona. She doesn't usually get up until after eight.'

'I know what time she gets up,' she retorted, facing him reluctantly. 'And I think you understand perfectly well what I mean. Just because you regard your stepmother's assistants as fair game—'

'What?' He gasped, the injustice of the remark catching him on the raw. 'I don't regard my stepmother's assistants as fair game,' he protested, hardly addressing the insult in his eagerness to defend himself. For God's sake, what was she implying? That Kristin Spencer had lost her job because of him?

She seemed a little uncomfortable now, perhaps realising that she, too, had overstepped the mark. Dammit, what had Catriona been telling her? he wondered. That he was to blame for her own feelings of insecurity?

'Did Catriona tell you that?' he demanded, not letting her move past him, his fingers about her forearm as much a surprise to him as they obviously were to her. And, as her eyes widened uneasily, he prompted, 'Well?'

'I—no,' she conceded at last, apparently thinking better of pursuing it, and he was relieved. 'Um—not in so many words, anyway.'

That was almost as bad. 'In what words, then?' he queried dangerously. 'You can tell me. I'd like to know.'

She shivered then, the tremor that rippled over her body communicating itself to him through her skin. 'Perhaps—perhaps I made a mistake,' she mumbled, no longer so sure of herself. 'Please—you're hurting me, Mr Redding. Let me go.'

'Not yet.' His desire to make her admit she'd been lying was in no way abated, even if he was more aware of the smoothness of her skin and the slim bones that flexed beneath it than he wanted to be. 'Either Catriona made the accusation or she didn't. And if she didn't, why did you say she had?'

'I didn't actually say she had,' she protested huskily. 'I—her other assistant left so—so unexpectedly, and—and—'

'And you thought I was to blame.' He scowled.

'Why? Because I've attempted to be friendly? It couldn't be because Kristin couldn't do her job?'

'It could be...'

'But you don't think so?'

'I don't know what I think,' she said unhappily. 'If—if I've offended you, I'm sorry.'

'Yeah. So you should be,' he muttered, and this time he gave in to her now silent plea and released her. 'Go on,' he added. 'Don't let me detain you. Contrary to current opinion, I'm not that desperate for female company.'

Her face flamed at his words, the dark colour vying with the dark red of the hair at her temples. Because her skin was pale, the freckles that marked the bridge of her nose stood out in sharp relief, and although he told himself that she deserved it his conscience was pricking him just the same.

She was such a strange creature, so confident in some ways, so uncertain in others. It seemed obvious, despite her denial, that Catriona had warned her to stay clear of him. But whether she'd made the excuse of Kristin's behaviour, or their own unsatisfactory association, he couldn't be sure.

'You won't—' She was rubbing the place where his hand had gripped her arm now, her tongue making a nervous exploration of her lips as she struggled to find the words to say. 'You won't—say anything to—to Miss Redding? About my—indiscretion?' She darted a look at his face. 'Will you?'

Dominic passed an impatient hand over his damp hair. This was getting too heavy, he thought, realising that she was making him feel like a conspirator. The trouble was, the longer he was with her, the more intrigued by her he became, and, although he assured himself that it was just curiosity he felt, the awareness of her as a woman—an oddly sensual woman—wasn't entirely voluntary.

'No,' he said at last, his tone as curt now as hers had been earlier, and she offered him a rare smile.

'Thanks,' she said gratefully, groping for the tufted end of her braid and tossing it over her shoulder. 'Um— enjoy your walk.'

As if he was in any mood to take a casual stroll after their bewildering confrontation, he thought as she followed the path up from the beach and disappeared into the garden. He felt angry now; angry, and strangely frustrated. Making her that promise was not what he'd wanted to do.

Catriona caught up with him that evening.

Instead of going back to the house as he'd intended, Dominic had collected his motorbike from the garage, and spent the rest of the day at Webb's Cove. Situated near Somerset Bridge, which was a local beauty spot, the boatyard and its small marina provided anchorage for a variety of craft. The coastline of the island was scalloped with small bays and inlets just like this one, and Webb's Cove was popular with the locals, some of whom moored charter craft in the basin.

When Dominic was a kid, he used to think that that was what he'd like to do when he grew up. The idea of sailing tourists around the islands all day had sounded very pleasant, but his father had soon put a stop to that. His son was not going to become a beach bum. He had an entirely different future in mind.

However, Lawrence Redding had enjoyed sailing, though he'd seldom made time to indulge his hobby, and when Dominic was fifteen he'd bought him a dinghy and taught him how to sail. Since then, Dominic had had several different craft, and with the advances in technology the necessity of a crew was no longer a factor. These days, the yacht was his bolt hole, the place he went when he needed an escape. Which was happening more and more often lately, he admitted. It was as if the older he got, the more problematic his life became.

Consequently, he'd spent a not altogether relaxed afternoon oiling canvas and shining brass. His boat— *Nightwing*—had benefited from the attention, no doubt, but the twin-masted vessel was only a diversion. Sooner or later, he'd known he had to go back to the house at Copperhead Bay.

The man who ran the boatyard, a huge barrel of a man called Max Erskine, had come to pay his respects, and Dominic had enjoyed their conversation. It was easy to talk about tides and reefs, and the ecological advantages of racing under sail. But when Max had turned the conversation to his father Dominic had felt like a hypocrite. How could he care about his father, when he was thinking of going to bed with his widow?

He'd ridden back to the house around six o'clock, and was in his apartment, preparing to take a shower, when someone had knocked at the door. Expecting it to be Samuel or one of the other servants, Dominic had called, 'Come in,' and then could have bitten out his tongue when Catriona opened the door.

'So here you are!' she exclaimed, coming into the room and closing the door, and leaning back somewhat triumphantly against it. 'I've been looking for you all afternoon. You might have let me know you were going out.'

'You're not my keeper, Cat.'

Dominic buttoned the waistband of his jeans, realising as he did so that it was a kind of protest. He resented Catriona feeling that she had the right to come here; he resented her presumption that he owed anything to her.

'Aren't I?' she asked now, her lips pursing in a *moue* of distaste. 'I rather thought I was, darling. You haven't forgotten who owns this house?'

Dominic's mouth hardened. 'No, I haven't forgotten,' he said coolly. 'And if you want me to leave you've only to say the word. I've got to get back to New York this week anyway. I don't suppose it matters which day I go.'

'Of course it matters!' Abandoning any pretence of condemnation, Catriona pushed away from the door and came towards him. 'Darling, you don't seem to understand—I've been—worried about you. You went out first thing this morning, and no one's heard from you since.'

So Miss Harris hadn't mentioned the fact that she'd seen him, he reflected dourly. Well, she wouldn't, would she? She was terrified of threatening her own position.

'I've been at the boatyard,' he conceded, after a moment, making no effort to respond to the caressing hand Catriona had laid on his arm. 'I had things to do. I didn't know I had to report my movements first.'

Catriona's lips tightened. 'We were supposed to be having breakfast together.'

'Were we?'

'You know we were.' Catriona was making a valiant effort to keep her temper. 'Instead of which, I was obliged to keep Miss Harris company.' She paused. 'I'm not at all sure that arrangement is going to work out.'

Dominic stiffened. 'What arrangement?'

'Miss Harris,' said Catriona testily, letting go of his arm and pressing her palms together. 'There's something about her...' She shook her head. 'I'm—not altogether sure she can be trusted.'

'Why not?'

Dominic's eyes had narrowed, and Catriona gave him a somewhat petulant look. 'Well,' she said, spreading her hands, 'you must have noticed. She's far too accommodating to be true!'

Dominic closed his eyes. He thought he had heard this one before. 'For God's sake,' he exclaimed, 'you're surely not implying she's another Kristin? Why can't she just be conscientious and nothing else?'

'Oh, I'm not implying she's like Kristin.' Catriona sounded almost amused. 'Dear me, Kristin was an attractive girl; even I could see that. She had some reason to feel that—that people might be interested in her. She was used to masculine admiration. Miss Harris, I'm sure, has no such pretensions.'

'You don't think so?'

As soon as the words were out, Dominic knew he shouldn't have said them, but Catriona's complete dismissal of Jaime as an attractive woman had caught him curiously on the raw.

'No.' Catriona regarded him impatiently now. 'For heaven's sake, have you looked at her? Really looked at her? She has *freckles*, Dominic! And that hair of hers is such an ugly colour! And her clothes—my God! I don't know where she gets them. She certainly doesn't care about how she looks.'

'Perhaps she thinks there are more important things in life,' remarked Dominic coolly, aware that he was compounding his original mistake. 'I—think she's quite attractive. Physically, she's a lot like you.'

'Like me!'

Catriona was horrified and, although when Dominic had made the remark his motives had been purely malicious, the sudden awareness that he had not been lying struck him squarely in the face.

Jaime Harris did remind him of Catriona.

He frowned. It wasn't immediately obvious, perhaps, which was why it had never occurred to him before. Certainly, their colouring was different, and there was no doubt that Catriona knew how to make the most of her good points, and Jaime didn't. The resemblance, such as it was, was a subtle thing, composed of shape and movement. They both walked with a loose-limbed elegance for such tall women; they both tilted their heads in the same enquiring way.

If there was more, he couldn't yet put his finger on

it. But it explained why he had felt that strange familiarity when he was with Jaime, he thought. It wasn't that they had met before, or that he had known her in some previous existence. It was simply that he had seen traces of his stepmother in her.

'You can't be serious!' Catriona was protesting now, and Dominic realised he would have to deal with the furore his careless words had created.

'All I meant was that you're both of a similar height and build,' he said, knowing he could not voice his real feelings. 'And, in any case, I don't think having freckles is such a crime.'

'But to say that we're alike.' Catriona gazed at him with wounded eyes. 'I can't believe you could be so cruel!'

Dominic sighed. 'It wasn't meant to be cruel,' he said wearily, giving in to her silent appeal and pulling her towards him. 'It was merely an observation. That was all.'

'Well, don't make those kind of observations in the future,' said Catriona, winding her arms about his neck. 'Oh, darling, you don't know how much I need you. When are we going to be together?'

CHAPTER FIVE

JAIME put the flat of her hand on top of her head, feeling the heat that was penetrating the thickness of her hair and causing the skin of her scalp to prickle ominously. It was so hot—much hotter than she had anticipated when she'd first left the house. She should have swallowed her pride and asked Catriona if she could borrow the Toyota, as Dominic Redding had suggested. Instead of which, she was standing at the bus stop on South Road, waiting for one of the pink buses that would take her into Hamilton.

It had been a ten-minute walk from the gates of Catriona's property, along Copperhead Lane to Salt Kettle Corner, where she was now waiting, and her T-shirt and shorts were sticking to her. In addition to which, the sun was giving her a slight headache, adding to her discomfort.

Of course, she hadn't expected to be given the afternoon off. She had been working for Catriona for a week now, and her timetable had seldom varied. Mornings were spent either transcribing the previous day's notes or dealing with some of the multitude of letters that Catriona received from her readers, while afternoons usually entailed a discussion of the work she had done, with Catriona detailing any alterations she wanted.

There were variations, of course, but Jaime was seldom free before four o'clock in the afternoon, and although she had come here with very clear intentions of what she wanted to do somehow her own needs were always being superseded by Catriona's. Besides, she still wasn't sure whether she wanted to stay or not, and it didn't seem wise to create problems for herself.

Today was different. Today, Catriona had dismissed her at lunchtime, with the suggestion that she take the opportunity to go into town. Jaime was given the distinct impression that her employer wanted her out of the house, and in her opinion that could only mean one thing. Catriona and Dominic intended to spend the afternoon together, and they wanted no voyeurs—unwilling or otherwise—to discourage their intimacy.

Jaime had no objections to leaving the house. Indeed she would prefer not to be a witness to their lovemaking, and it was this as much as anything that had stopped her from asking to use the Toyota. She preferred not to risk another encounter with Dominic Redding, and although it was four days since she had seen him on the beach she had succeeded in avoiding another confrontation.

Not least because he was avoiding her too, she suspected, remembering the morning she had seen him emerging like some pagan deity from the waves with an unwilling shiver of apprehension. Dear God, she had nearly died when she'd realised he wasn't wearing any swimming shorts, and she'd prayed the sand would just open up and swallow her whole.

Of course, it hadn't, and she'd been forced to stand there like an idiot, waiting for the moment when his eyes would alight on her cringing figure. God! She shivered again, in spite of the heat. He had been completely shameless. He hadn't cared that she had seen him. On the contrary, he'd behaved as if nothing untoward had happened, had actually invited her to go swimming with him, besides.

She felt a sense of incredulity. She could imagine Catriona's reaction to hearing that. Which was why she had said what she had, practically accusing him of trying to seduce her, when what she'd really wanted to do was ask him when he'd started the affair with his father's wife. Was he completely amoral? And didn't he care that Catriona was practically old enough to be his mother?

Such thoughts were not conducive to a quiet mind, and Jaime had spent the last few days trying to come to terms with what she'd discovered. It didn't help that all her efforts to make friendly overtures towards Catriona had been countered. The woman didn't even seem to like her, and Jaime was very much afraid she felt the same.

So why was she staying on…?

She shook her head impatiently, turning to stare down the road, which seemed to shift and waver before her aching eyes. She knew it was only the heat that was causing the shimmering effect, but she hadn't eaten since early that morning, and the unsteadiness was making her feel sick.

To divert herself, she determinedly thought about the manuscript she was typing. Although Catriona had been partway through the new novel when Jaime had started working for her, the alterations and additions that had been made to the original typescript meant that Jaime was familiar with every aspect of the story. It was a new departure for Catriona, she'd discovered—a modern novel, instead of the period pieces she usually wrote. And although the idea of a failed businessman coming to the island to escape his creditors, and helping the heroine to make a success of the run-down hotel she'd inherited, was promising, in Catriona's hands it was threatening to be her first mistake.

The trouble was, Catriona's strength lay in the sparkling dialogue she usually had between the hero and heroine, and her attempt to put modern words into modern mouths was proving difficult. The conversations Jaime had typed were definitely dated, and despite her skill at narrative Catriona's historical pedigree was showing through.

Which might account for the uncertainty of her temper, reflected Jaime thoughtfully, trying to be charitable.

Certainly, it had taken days to get one particular scene the way she wanted it, and even now Jaime guessed she wasn't content. Still, it wasn't part of her brief to offer criticism, even if Catriona had asked for it. She had the feeling that whatever advice she might offer Catriona would take exception to it.

A car went by, throwing up a cloud of dust, and Jaime wondered how much longer she was going to have to wait. According to Samuel, it was going to take the better part of an hour to get into Hamilton anyway. Although the distance wasn't great, the buses stopped to pick up and put down passengers every few yards.

She wondered if she should turn back. Perhaps she could slip into her rooms unnoticed, and spend the afternoon lying on her bed. She was hungry, but that would pass. There was a bowl of fruit in her room, and she could manage with an apple or a mango. It would be so nice to get out of the heat and the constant glare of the sun.

She heard the sound of another vehicle and turned her face away from the road. It obviously wasn't one of the buses, which made a much more distinctive sound, and she was weary of watching other vehicles speed by her. Though perhaps 'speed' wasn't quite the word, she conceded, pressing the back of her hand against her damp forehead. No one drove very fast, even if the twenty miles an hour speed limit wasn't always adhered to.

'What the hell are you doing?'

Her first realisation that the vehicle had stopped was the disturbingly familiar sound of Dominic's voice demanding an explanation. She turned, most unwillingly, to find him leaning across the front seat of the open-topped Toyota, his eyes dark with impatience at the sight of her wilting figure.

'I'm—waiting for the bus,' she declared at last, wishing she had the nerve to tell him to mind his own business. What the hell did he think she was doing? She wasn't waiting at the bus stop for fun.

'Get in,' he ordered immediately, releasing the catch and pushing open the passenger-side door. 'Didn't Cat tell you I'd be back at lunchtime? I said you were free to borrow the car.'

Jaime hesitated. 'It doesn't matter,' she said, not wanting to admit she hadn't asked her. And then, to her relief, she saw the bus she had been waiting for approaching. 'I—wanted to get the bus. Samuel says it's a good way to see more of the island.'

'Samuel was born here,' said Dominic dampeningly, making no effort to drive away. 'Come on. Get in, before you fall in. I don't know who you think you're kidding, but you're as pale as a ghost.'

'I'm all right,' she insisted, and moved towards the back of the car, with every intention of flagging down the bus.

'No, you're not,' he snarled, and before she could prevent it he had vaulted out of the car and taken hold of her. 'Don't make me lose my temper. I'll take you into Hamilton, if that's where you want to go.'

Jaime swayed a little unsteadily. 'There's no need,' she said, trying not very successfully to get away. But his hand gripping her shoulder felt so heavy, and she didn't feel as if she had the strength to resist.

And while she was prevaricating the bus she had waited for so patiently sailed by without stopping. 'Damn,' she said, gazing after it, and Dominic gave her a sardonic look.

'Is that the best you can do?' he asked, leading her inexorably back to the vehicle. 'Don't worry about it. I can get you there much quicker.'

Jaime sniffed. 'Maybe I don't want to get there much quicker,' she mumbled, but she subsided into the front seat of the car anyway. 'Have you been following me?'

'As if.' Dominic gestured in the direction from which

he had come, and walked round the car to get in beside her. His hairy thigh was only inches from hers as he coiled his impressive length behind the wheel. It was too hot to wear trousers, and like her he was wearing shorts: denims this time, the well-washed cloth moulding the powerful muscles with a sensual attention to detail. 'I've just been down to the Southampton Princess. A pal of mine is spending a couple of weeks there with his girl-friend.'

Jaime pressed her lips together, determining not to comment, but curiosity got the better of her. 'The Southampton Princess?' she echoed as he reached for the ignition, and Dominic gave her a sidelong glance.

'It's a hotel,' he explained. 'One of the best on the island. You should take a trip there some time. There are shops and restaurants, and they'll even teach you to scuba-dive, if you need the exercise.'

'Mmm.'

Jaime was noncommittal. She had the feeling she was not going to be here long enough to see everything she'd like to see. Today might be an exception, but her employer would not approve if she could see her now.

'So—Hamilton, right?' said Dominic, looking at her expectantly, and Jaime felt an overwhelming sense of weariness. She had been so enthusiastic about the outing when she'd left the house, but now she just felt tired—and a little dispirited, too.

'I'm not sure,' she said, after a moment, realising she was being contrary, but not at all sure she wanted—let alone *ought*—to let him take her. 'I—as a matter of fact, I've got a headache,' she admitted. That was unhappily true. 'Perhaps I should just go back to the house and spend the afternoon on my bed.'

'Alone?'

Dominic was only teasing her. She knew that. Yet she couldn't deny the frisson of anticipation that rippled down her spine at his careless words. But it wasn't her he was thinking of going to bed with, she reminded herself. If he wanted that kind of diversion, it would be with his stepmother, and her awareness of that alliance brought a line of disapproval to her lips.

'If you could just help me to catch up with the bus again,' she said stiffly, and Dominic gave her a curious look.

'I thought you just said you had a headache.'

Jaime licked her lips. 'It's not a bad headache,' she argued, realising he wouldn't believe her if she denied it completely. 'I'll be perfectly all right once I get to Hamilton. I probably need a drink.'

Dominic's look hardened, and then, without another word, he put the car into gear and did a complete U-turn on the road. Instead of driving towards Hamilton, they were now heading in the opposite direction. Not down Copperhead Lane, but sticking to the South Road, which she knew, from the guidebook she had bought before she'd come here, led to the parishes of Southampton and Somerset.

'What are you doing?' she exclaimed, looking back over her shoulder, not exactly apprehensive, but not entirely comfortable either. 'This isn't the way to Hamilton, is it? Are you going a different way home?' And then, when she saw a sign on her left indicating another turn-off for Copperhead Bay, she asked, 'Shouldn't we have turned down there?'

'No.'

Dominic was non-communicative now, and Jaime gave him a nervous look. 'I—didn't you say Ca—Miss Redding was expecting you back? It's nearly half past one, you know.'

'So?'

Jaime chewed on her lower lip. 'So—isn't she going to worry, if you don't turn up?'

Dominic's mouth took on a mocking slant. 'Catriona doesn't worry,' he said. 'Not about anyone else, that is.'

Jaime suppressed an inward groan. She didn't need this, she told herself. She didn't want to have to leave Bermuda on anyone's terms but her own. But if Catriona found out about this—whatever it was—she'd have the perfect excuse to dismiss her. She would never believe Jaime's excuses, not when she considered Dominic was never to blame.

'Please,' she said, despising herself for the begging note that had entered her voice. 'I want to go back.'

'Why?' He didn't look at her as he spoke. 'I thought your headache was feeling better.'

'Well—it is.' Jaime paused, not knowing which admission would damn her most. The truth was, the breeze had cooled her temples, and the throbbing had almost gone.

'Good.' Dominic's long fingers swung the wheel as the open-topped vehicle negotiated another bend. 'Do you like the view? That's West Whale Bay. It's a popular beach with the locals.'

Jaime expelled her breath on a long sigh. The view was quite spectacular, of course. South Road took an elevated route, with the beautiful coves and bays that were scattered along its coastline spread out below. The headlands were green and, in some cases, wooded, with bushes of cape myrtle and oleander providing vivid splashes of colour. Between the bays, rocks rose dark, or coated with mosses, while the ocean was green where it was shallowest and dark blue where it was not.

The night she had arrived at Copperhead Bay, she'd paid little attention to her surroundings. She'd been too anxious then, too apprehensive that Catriona might not offer her the job. She was apprehensive now, she supposed, though for different reasons, but it would have been impossible not to marvel at the scenery as they passed.

'Where are you taking me?' she asked, pressing her hands together in her lap. This was crazy, she thought incredulously. He didn't really want to be with her. He was doing this to antagonise Catriona, she decided. And she didn't want to play any part in their games.

'Well, as you didn't seem particularly desperate to go shopping, I thought you might like to have lunch with me,' he declared at last. 'Oh, and by the way, this is Somerset Bridge. I dare say you've heard of it.'

Jaime caught her breath. 'You're not serious!'

'Yes, I am.' He nodded infuriatingly. 'This is Somerset Bridge. It's another famous beauty—'

'You're not serious about me having lunch with you?' she overrode him impatiently. 'D—Mr Redding, you know your stepmother is expecting you back. And—and I want to go into Hamilton. Um—I've got some personal things I want to buy.'

He glanced sideways at her. 'You nearly said Dominic then, didn't you?' he teased her mockingly. He shrugged. 'In any case, there are shops in Somerset village. You can probably get anything you need there.'

Jaime breathed deeply. 'But what about Miss Redding?'

'What about Miss Redding?' His expression sobered. 'Miss Redding can entertain herself for once. She's not my keeper, you know.'

'Isn't she?'

The words just slipped out, and Dominic bestowed a brooding look on her. 'No,' he said flatly. 'Whatever you may have heard to the contrary. Now—' He paused. 'Are you hungry or aren't you? Or do you really want me to take you back?'

She knew what she should say, what she *ought* to say, but they were driving past a small harbour now, and she was unwillingly aware that she didn't want to go back yet. 'Um—yes,' she mumbled, barely audibly. And then, his scowl alerting her to the fact that he'd misunderstood her, she added hurriedly, 'I mean—I am hungry.' She paused. 'Where were you thinking of having lunch?'

Dominic's expression cleared. 'We can eat here, in Somerset, if you like. Or alternatively we could buy some food and have it on the boat.' And at her startled look he explained, 'I've got a yacht. It's moored in Webb's Cove. We passed the turn-off just a few minutes ago.'

Jaime's lips parted. 'I—well—which would you prefer?'

'The boat, I think.' Dominic surveyed the tourists who were milling about the narrow streets. 'The restaurants can be pretty busy at this time of year.'

And they might encounter someone Dominic knew, thought Jaime shrewdly, although as he was bound to know other boatowners, too, that didn't quite ring true. She frowned, and then, deciding it wasn't her concern, she resolved to stop worrying. She'd committed herself now, and there was no going back on her promise. She tried to ignore the fact that Catriona might object.

CHAPTER SIX

A HALF-HOUR later, Dominic parked the car at the small marina. As Jaime had expected, there were a number of other yachtsmen about, sculling backwards and forwards between the different craft that were moored in the basin, or standing around talking to a man who might be the owner of the small boatyard that catered to the sailing community's needs. There was the scent of salt and seaweed, and a strong aroma of kerosene, as well as the smells of paint and other compounds used for repairing damaged hulls.

They had bought shrimp and salad at the small supermarket, as well as cheese, and freshly baked bread, and a tub of creamy butter. Dominic had also purchased some strawberries, the biggest Jaime had ever seen, and a ripe, juicy mango, to have as a dessert.

It was a day out of time, and Jaime refused to let thoughts of Carlona's anger spoil it. Besides, she assured herself, they were doing nothing wrong. Having lunch with a man did not constitute an unforgivable sin, and if her employer did find out, so what? She wasn't afraid of the woman, for God's sake!

'Hey, Dominic!' The man who Jaime had guessed owned the boatyard saw them, and, leaving the men he had been talking with, he sauntered over. He was a broad man, enormously big and fat, his waistband almost invisible beneath his overhanging belly. 'I didn't expect to see you again today,' he added, his eyes flickering to Jaime and back again. 'Aren't you going to introduce me to your friend?'

Dominic's mouth took on a wry slant. 'Sure,' he said,

his hand curving round Jaime's bare elbow with disturbing familiarity. 'Jaime, this is Max Erskine. He runs this place and he likes to know everything that's going on.'

Jaime's smile was strained, as much from the awareness of Dominic's hard fingers gripping her flesh, and his casual use of her first name, as from any apprehension at being singled out in this way. 'Hello,' she said, unable to hide her uneasiness. 'It's very nice to meet you.'

'Likewise,' declared Max, smiling, though his dark eyes were intent. 'You're a lucky man, Dom, my friend,' he averred, his gaze moving back to the other man. 'You're surrounded by pretty ladies.'

Hardly pretty, thought Jaime drily, not at all deluded about her appearance. She'd been told her eyes were her best feature, and her skin was good, but no one would call her 'pretty'. She was pleasant-looking, and that was when she was at her best.

'Aren't I though?' Dominic's response was gallant, and Max Erskine ran a huge hand over his shaved head.

'Some men have all the luck,' he commented, his smile too sincere not to be genuine. 'Give me a call if you need anything,' he added. His eyes moved mischievously back to Jaime. 'Not that I think you will.'

'Sorry about that,' remarked Dominic ruefully as they climbed aboard the small dinghy that was apparently going to take them out to the yacht. He started the outboard motor. 'Max considers himself quite a ladies' man, believe it or not.'

'Hmm.'

Jaime didn't quite know how to answer him, and diverted herself by wondering which of the craft moored in the small basin was Dominic's. There were several larger craft, although some of them were motor cruisers. Jaime knew little enough about sailing, but she did know that a yacht should have a mast.

More than one mast, she saw at once, when Dominic

brought the dinghy alongside a gleaming hull. Dear heaven, she thought, gazing up at the smooth sweep of fibreglass, how on earth was she expected to get on board?

To her relief, it proved to be quite easy. Dominic guided the dinghy round to the stern, where a small diving platform rose only a short distance above the water. It was where the dinghy was usually moored, he said as he released the handrail and helped her onto the yacht. 'Welcome aboard,' he added. '*Nightwing* and I are delighted to have your company.'

'*Nightwing*?' Jaime repeated the word experimentally. 'Is that what the boat is called?'

'Mmm.' Dominic nodded, securing the handrail again, and gesturing for her to go forward. 'I was going to call her *Nightwind*, but my hand slipped.'

Jaime's head jerked round. 'Are you seri—?' she was beginning, when she saw his teasing face. 'Oh, I see you weren't,' she continued. 'It's quite unusual, anyway.'

'Like you,' said Dominic, surprising her, and when her face suffused with sudden colour he made an impatient sound. 'Like now,' he said. 'I can't remember the last time I met a woman who still knew how to blush.'

'It's not an advantage,' murmured Jaime uncomfortably, not quite sure what he meant. 'Um—it's a beautiful boat. Have you had it long?'

'*Her*,' he corrected her easily. 'Have I had *her* long? For some reason, boats are always female. Because they can be unpredictable, I suppose.'

'I did know that,' said Jaime, realising she had reached the steps that led down into the cabin. 'And I think it's more likely because men think they can master them. They find it harder with their own sex.'

'Are you a feminist, Miss Harris?' he mocked her, pushing aside the housing, and vaulting down into the living area below. He looked up at her. 'Do you need some help, or can you manage? I wouldn't want to be accused of taking advantage of the situation.'

Jaime pressed her lips together. 'I can manage,' she said, aware that she wasn't quite sure she could handle Dominic in this mood. All her preconceptions of the kind of man he was were being sorely tested, and although on the other occasions they had been together she had kept a distinct barrier between them his humour was infectious. She couldn't prevent herself from smiling, too, and he was evidently pleased with her response.

'Much better,' he said as she reached the lower level, and she decided there was no point in treating him like the enemy today. 'What do you think?' he appended, inviting her to look around. 'This is the main cabin, and that's the galley. There are a couple of sleeping berths with heads—bathrooms?—through there.'

'Do you mean for'ard?' she enquired cheekily, earning a lazy grin, and for a moment the dangers she was courting loomed large before her.

'Yeah, that's what I meant,' he agreed, dumping the bag of groceries on the drainer in the small galley. 'You know,' he continued, 'I like you better when you're not constantly looking for a fight.'

Jaime caught her breath. 'I've never looked for a fight,' she protested. 'Only...'

'Only—what?'

'Well...' She allowed her fingers to graze the surface of the gleaming teak table that was bolted between two velvet-cushioned benches, wondering what on earth she could say to justify herself. 'I—I just think Miss Redding wouldn't approve of me—' What? *What?* '—wasting your time.'

Dominic came to brace his hip against a marble-topped unit. 'Why do I get the feeling that's not what you were going to say?' he queried drily, squashing the sense of relief she'd felt at her sudden inspiration. 'That's the second time you've implied that Catriona has some prior claim on my—what shall we say?—actions? Exactly what kind of a relationship do you think she and I have?'

Oh, God! Jaime's face flamed. 'I—um—it's nothing to do with me,' she muttered, and Dominic inclined his head.

'No, it's not,' he agreed flatly. 'So let's agree to leave my private life alone, shall we? What goes on between my stepmother and myself need not concern you. Right?'

Jaime swallowed. 'Right.'

'Good.' He turned back into the galley and extracted a bottle of wine from the small fridge. 'Let's have a toast to new beginnings, hmm?'

'Fine.'

The word was too thin, and Jaime struggled to gather her composure, and behave as he would expect someone in her position to behave. She should be flattered, after all, that he was bothering to entertain her, and if she had been the woman he imagined her to be she wouldn't allow any doubts about his association with her employer to interfere with her own enjoyment. Of course, Kristin Spencer's abrupt dismissal might have given her pause, but the other girl would probably have been so bemused by Dominic's attentions that she'd have fooled herself into thinking she could handle it...

'You're looking very serious again.' Dominic had poured the wine into two slender wine glasses now, and was offering one to her. 'Tell me, is it just me, or are you naturally averse to the opposite sex?'

'I don't know what you mean.'

It was hard having to think on her feet all the time, and Dominic's expression seemed to reveal he was even more astute than she'd thought. 'Of course you do,' he contradicted her softly. 'Do I intimidate you, or what?'

'You do when you say things like that,' she countered quickly, realising she was probably wasting a glorious opportunity to learn more about Catriona by being nervous. If only she weren't so aware of him as a man. His behaviour was blinding her to the real reason why she was here.

'Okay.' Touching his glass to the one he had put into her nervous fingers, he seemed to relent. 'I promise I'll be good if you will.' He grinned. 'Why don't you lay the table while I put out the food? You'll find everything you need in the cupboard there.'

Breathing a little more easily, Jaime did as she was bid, setting out heavy silver knives and forks on linen place mats that had been hand-painted with island scenes.

'These are nice,' she said, glad of having something uncontroversial to say, and Dominic swallowed the mouthful of wine he had just taken before saying,

'Yes. They're painted by a friend of mine who lives in St George's.' He paused to take a lemon from the fridge. 'That's at the other end of the island. You'll have to meet her some time.'

Jaime sipped her own drink. 'Her?'

'Jill Jackson,' said Dominic, giving a rueful smile. 'Another woman, I'm afraid. But this one's married.'

Jaime's lips compressed, but she made no comment, and presently Dominic emerged from the galley carrying two plates containing a delicious shrimp salad. 'There's mayonnaise, if you want it,' he said, 'though I'm afraid it's not home-made. Sophie's mayonnaise is always fresh, but I didn't know I was going to need any today.'

'This is fine as it is,' Jaime assured him, taking the seat he indicated, and viewing her plate with real enjoyment. She squeezed lemon juice over the shrimp as Dominic sliced the bread he had brought to the table on a pine board. 'I do appreciate this, you know,' she added awkwardly. 'It was too hot to go shopping, really.'

'So why were you going?' asked Dominic reasonably,

tearing apart the slice of bread he had put on his own plate and adding a thick layer of creamy yellow butter.

'Oh—' Jaime was loath to admit it, but it had to be said. 'Um—Miss Redding suggested it. She—she said she wouldn't need me this afternoon, and that perhaps I'd like to go into town.'

'I see.' Dominic refilled her wine glass and his own, and then considered his plate. 'Well…' He too seemed determined not to say anything provocative. 'It's lucky I came along as I did.'

'Mmm.' Jaime realised her response sounded doubtful and to cover herself she looked determinedly through the window beside her. 'This is such a beautiful cove,' she said, feeling the boat moving gently beneath her. 'I don't suppose I'd have known of its existence if you hadn't brought me here.'

'No.'

Dominic's response was neutral enough, but she wondered somewhat uneasily what he was really thinking. Was he regretting the impulse that had caused him to invite her? Was he already anticipating Catriona's reaction if—*when*—she found out?

'Does—er—does Miss Redding enjoy sailing?' she ventured, deciding anything was better than trying to guess his mood. 'I—wondered if she went sailing with your father,' she added hurriedly as his dark eyes rose to fix her with a penetrating look.

'No,' he said at last, laying his knife aside, and using his fork to spear a slice of tomato. 'No, Cat never goes sailing. Like her namesake, she's not fond of water.'

'Oh.' Jaime forced a smile, and concentrated on her own plate. But the knowledge that Catriona was unlikely to have slept with Dominic here was disturbingly welcome. The image of them together was far too acute.

'My father seldom had time to go sailing,' Dominic continued, surprising her. 'He was what I guess you'd call a workaholic. Unlike me, he never liked to delegate, which is something that nowadays is considered an important attribute of any business.'

Jaime hesitated. 'Had—er—had your parents been married long? When your father died, I mean?'

'My mother died when I was six,' Dominic told her succinctly. 'I never considered Cat as her replacement. I was sixteen when my father married again.'

'I see.' Jaime could feel the colour creeping into her neck again and forced it back. 'So they were married for quite a long time, weren't they?' She ignored Dominic's sardonic expression. 'Um—how did they meet?'

Dominic's eyes were quizzical. 'Are you really interested? Or is this a ploy to stop me from provoking you?'

'I am interested.' The colour poured into her face now unabated. 'I'm curious about—about when Miss Redding started writing her books.'

'Okay.' Dominic swallowed a mouthful of his wine, and then returned his gaze to her flushed face. 'They met when her London agent sent one of her manuscripts to my father's company. You may have heard of Goldman and Redding. My grandfather, Lawrence Redding—my father's namesake—and Stanley Goldman started the firm in 1922.'

'How romantic!' Only Jaime knew how ironic those words were. 'And your father published it, and it was an immediate success!'

'Not quite.' Dominic set down his glass again. 'As a matter of fact, he never did publish that original manuscript. Cat—she called herself Catriona Markham in those days—used to write detective novels. My father suggested she try historical fiction instead.'

Jaime swallowed. 'Catriona Markham,' she said, managing to keep the tremor out of her voice. 'I don't think I know that name.'

'No, well—that's really not surprising.' Dominic grimaced. 'The three detective novels she wrote never saw the light of day. That was why her agent sent the new manuscript to Goldman and Redding. In the hope that an American publisher might find it more appealing.'

'And did they?'

'Unfortunately not.' Dominic paused. 'But my father must have considered it had some merit, because he asked if he could meet the author, and Catriona and he were married six months later.'

Jaime caught her breath. 'Just like that.'

'So it seems.' Dominic shrugged. 'That was about twenty years ago, if you're calculating. I'm thirty-six, and Catriona's almost forty-five.'

'Almost—forty-five?'

Jaime could barely get the words out, and Dominic misunderstood her shocked response. 'Yeah, she doesn't look it, does she?' he said, cutting himself more bread. 'She was considerably younger than my father.'

Not that much younger, Jaime wanted to say bitterly, but she kept her mouth shut. Nevertheless, it helped to explain their relationship. Dominic had obviously considered she was more his contemporary than his father's.

Aware that Dominic was watching her now, possibly waiting for her to say something more, Jaime sought refuge in her wine glass. Forty-five! she thought. It was incredible. Catriona had to have been over thirty, twenty years ago.

Apparently deciding she was waiting for him to continue, Dominic went on. 'She wrote her first novel after they were married. She always says my father pointed her in the right direction.'

Jaime nodded, trying to remain calm. As far as Dominic was concerned, this was what she was interested in. She had to remember she was supposed to be a fan! Her interest in Catriona had to sound purely objective.

Realising she had to say something, she chose the least personal thing she could think of. 'And—and he encouraged her to write—romantic novels?'

'Some might say he was the *reason* she started writing romantic novels,' observed Dominic drily. 'After all, she hadn't had much love in her life up to that point.'

Jaime stiffened. 'Did she say that?' she demanded. And then, anxious that she might have betrayed herself, she added, 'I mean—well, she had been married before, hadn't she?' She took a breath as she saw his doubtful expression. 'Hadn't she?'

Dominic frowned. 'If she had I've never heard of it,' he declared, regarding her curiously. 'I believe she'd worked as a nanny before they met.' He frowned. 'What's wrong? You're looking very pale all of a sudden. Don't tell me you're feeling seasick. This is just a gentle swell.'

Jaime struggled to gather herself. 'I—no,' she mumbled, taking another sip of her wine. 'I'm not seasick. At least, I don't think I am anyway,' she appended, forcing a smile. 'I just felt—dizzy, for a moment. It's gone now. I feel fine.'

'Well, you don't look fine,' said Dominic flatly. He glanced about him. 'It's stuffy down here. I suggest we finish the wine on deck. What do you think?'

'All right.'

Jaime didn't care where they went, so long as she had a few minutes to recover her scattered senses. As she followed Dominic up the steps, she wondered if the woman had ever told the truth in her life. It was obvious that she'd hidden the fact that she'd been married and it hurt to think that her own existence had been denied.

It was hot on deck, but the sun was slatted by the sails of a yacht moored close by, and the breeze off the water made the heat bearable. Dominic added cushions to the polished seats in the stern and raised the canopy, and Jaime drew her legs up onto the seat and wrapped her arms about them. For all her misgivings, she couldn't help but feel a sense of wonder at her surroundings. It was a new experience for her to feel a part of what was going on.

'Better?' enquired Dominic, stretching his length beside her, and Jaime gave him a grateful look.

'Much better,' she conceded, tossing her braid over her shoulder. She took her glass from him, and sipped it appreciatively. 'I suppose I ought to be thinking of going back.'

'Why?'

Dominic's arm was along the back of the seat, and Jaime was intensely conscious of its nearness. Although he was wearing a shirt today, the sleeves were short, exposing his brown arms. Muscled arms, she noticed nervously, lightly defined with fine, dark hair.

'Well—because,' she answered him, not altogether satisfactorily. 'We can't stay here all afternoon.'

'I don't intend that we should,' he told her, startling her anew. 'I thought we might sail round the point into Spiny Bay. Have you ever been snorkelling? If not, I can recommend it. The underwater landscape is just as fascinating as the island itself.'

Jaime stared at him. 'I don't know how to—sail a boat,' she objected uneasily, aware that that was the least of her worries.

'You don't have to.' Dominic was coolly relaxed.

'And—I don't have a bathing suit,' she added stiffly, already colouring at the prospect of his response. She had no intention of shedding her inhibitions as well as her common sense.

'No problem.' Dominic pushed himself up from his seat. But the relief she felt at his departure was short-lived. 'We can get one from Max's shop,' he responded calmly. 'The chandlery stocks everything you need.'

Jaime tightened her arms about her updrawn knees. 'I—I don't know.'

'I do,' said Dominic, rocking on his heels. 'You stay here. I shan't be long.'

Before she could do more than utter a weak protest, he had vaulted into the dinghy, released the painter, and started the outboard motor. She turned to kneel on the bench seat as he sped away towards the jetty, wondering what she'd do if he didn't come back.

She didn't have to wonder long. She had barely carried their glasses down to the galley, to rinse them in the small sink, when she heard the dinghy coming back. Her heart quickened its beat in spite of herself as the sudden rocking of the vessel warned her that Dominic was back on board. Then he came noisily down the stairwell, and tossed a plastic carrier onto the drainer.

'Go try it on,' he suggested, pulling a face at her efforts at domesticity. 'I didn't bring you here to wash dishes. You're supposed to be having fun.'

Jaime hesitated. 'Well, how much was it?' she asked, picking up the bag but making no effort to look inside, and Dominic heaved a frustrated sigh.

'Try it on first; then I'll tell you,' he told her flatly. 'Use one of the other cabins. I'm going to check on the fuel.'

Jaime blinked. 'But—I thought—I mean, isn't this a sailing vessel?'

'Of course.' Dominic's smile was indulgent now. 'But it's easier to use the engine to get out of the marina. You'll see. We'll make a sailor of you yet.'

CHAPTER SEVEN

LEAVING Jaime, Dominic went back up on deck and presently she felt the vessel vibrate as the engine started. It reassured her that he would not be coming back to check on her straight away, and, carrying the bag, she crossed the saloon and entered one of the sleeping compartments.

Like the main cabin, it was comfortably furnished, with a wide double berth, and end tables full of useful drawers. Above the bed were more cupboards, designed like an elaborate headboard, with floor-to-ceiling closets, and a vanity unit complete with mirrors.

She had been expecting him to have bought her a bikini—one of those skimpy two-piece suits that exposed more than they covered—but when she opened the bag she found Dominic had chosen a simple black maillot. It was strapless, it was true, and the legs were cut quite high, but compared to what she had anticipated it was almost conservative.

All the same, she thought she must be mad as she pulled her T-shirt and shorts on again over the swimsuit. She had come to the island to get to know Catriona Redding, not her stepson, and although she had learned more about her employer today than at any other time since she'd arrived the fact remained she was not here just to enjoy herself.

But she was enjoying herself.

And that scared her.

It would be ironic, she thought, stuffing her underwear into the carrier bag, if this trip turned out to have hidden dangers she hadn't even thought of. She didn't like the feeling that events were moving out of her control. She had always known exactly who she was and what she was doing, but suddenly she had doubts.

Until her father died...

But she didn't want to think about Robert Michaels now, and, expelling her breath with more care than confidence, she squared her shoulders and opened the door. She could handle this, she told herself. No, scrub that; she *had* to handle this. She wasn't an impressionable teenager, for heaven's sake. She'd dealt with men before.

She'd half expected Dominic to be waiting outside the door, but the relief she felt at finding the saloon empty was short-lived. As she stood there uncertainly, wondering what to do with the bag containing her underwear, he called down to her, and, thrusting it onto one of the padded benches, she climbed the stairs.

His expression when he saw her was almost comical. 'It didn't fit?' he asked in surprise as she joined him in the wheelhouse, and Jaime moved her shoulders in a gesture of assent.

'It did. It does,' she amended, easing herself onto the seat beside him. And, to divert her racing pulses from the fact that he'd removed his shirt in her absence, she added, 'Oh, I see we've left the marina already.'

Dominic was paying little attention to his surroundings. 'What do you mean—it fits?' he demanded, with some exasperation. 'So, why aren't you wearing it?'

Jaime kept her gaze on the wide expanse of ocean opening ahead of them. 'I am wearing it,' she replied, feeling the adrenaline surging through her veins. 'Oh, look!' Her breath caught in her throat. 'Aren't those rocks ahead?'

Dominic's head swung round automatically to check for any hazards, but his voice was just as impatient when he spoke. 'It's seaweed,' he said flatly. 'You can see it moving beneath the surface. These waters are shallow, but they're perfectly safe for this type of craft.'

'Oh, good.'

Jaime hunched her shoulders, managing to sound relieved, which wasn't difficult in the present circumstances. She was relieved to talk about something other than her appearance, though she guessed Dominic wasn't satisfied with her response.

However, for the next few minutes he was busy cutting the engine, and raising the sails. To Jaime, who had never sailed before, and whose knowledge, gleaned from movies, involved hauling on sheets and halyards, the hydraulic-powered system of rigging was a revelation. The sails unfurled so smoothly, catching the wind, and billowing above her head. The yacht seemed to lift in sympathy, and its previously pedestrian pace was forgotten. Like a bird, it seemed to take flight, gathering speed, and moving swiftly over the water.

In spite of herself, Jaime was enchanted by it. There was something magical about skimming across the ocean, the prow slicing a path between the waves, outstripping everything else in sight. Only when the hull tilted, as Dominic swung the craft about, did she clutch rather grimly at the housing. But she refused to let him think that she was apprehensive, and she surreptitiously dried her sweating palms on the seams of her shorts.

It took only minutes to round the headland, and before she knew what he was doing Dominic was lowering the mainsail, to tack into what she assumed was Spiny Bay. Before them, a stretch of white beach was backed by a wooded hillside, but Dominic dropped anchor some distance out from the shore.

The hydraulic winch disposed of the rest of the sails, and then the silence was almost deafening. All she could hear was the pull of the wind against the masts, and the sucking sound of the water as it lapped against the hull.

'What do you think?' Dominic asked eventually, and

Jaime took a moment to moisten her dry lips before replying.

'I think—it's beautiful,' she said honestly, unable to think of anything more original. But she was suddenly aware of how isolated they were, how far from anything—or anyone—she knew.

'Yes, it is, isn't it?' She stiffened as he rose to his feet, but all he did was cross the deck to look over the side. 'These waters are teeming with fish, you know, if you're still hungry.' He grimaced. 'I think I've got some tackle down below.'

It wasn't a serious observation, and Jaime stood up also, and forced herself to walk to the rail. 'Do you come here a lot?' she asked, despising her inability to think of anything witty to say, and Dominic's mouth turned down at the corners.

'When I need to,' he replied, somewhat enigmatically, and Jaime used his words to fuel her flagging contempt.

Yet when she looked at him it wasn't easy to sustain her resentment. He'd been kind to her—kinder than she deserved. It wasn't his fault that she was apprehensive. He had no idea who she really was.

'Aren't you going to ask me what I mean?' he enquired, after a moment, and Jaime was forced to give him a fleeting look.

'It's nothing to do with me,' she said, envying him his confidence. Was he implying it was difficult, carrying on an affair with his father's widow? She hoped he didn't expect her sympathy. She despised him—she despised both of them. But she couldn't help wondering how long it had been going on.

'That hasn't troubled you up till now,' he observed as she was striving for indifference, and her eyes widened indignantly at his words. 'Well, you've asked enough questions,' he pointed out. 'None of them relevant to your position.' He paused. 'I get the feeling you've judged me, and found me wanting.'

'That's ridiculous—'

'Is it?' Dominic surveyed her tense figure without remorse. 'You don't approve of my—friendship with my stepmother, do you? You can't blame me if I wonder why.'

'Well, it's not what you think,' declared Jaime automatically, and then winced at the mocking expression on his face. 'Oh, this is silly. I don't want to talk about it. We agreed to leave your—er—private affairs alone.'

'Affairs?' Dominic's tone mocked her. 'What an emotive word that is.' He moved a little closer to her along the rail. 'Have you had many affairs, Jaime? Are you perhaps an expert on what goes on? I can't believe I'm the first man to be fascinated by those often solemn—yet always intriguing—features. You're a curious mix of innocence and guile.'

Jaime's jaw dropped. 'Mr Redding—'

'Dominic.'

'Mr Redding, please; stop teasing me.'

'Teasing you?' To her horror, he lifted his hand to brush her cheek, and although all her instincts were screaming at her to move away from him her need to prove that it meant nothing to her kept her rooted to the spot. 'Who said I was teasing?' he continued, rubbing the pad of his thumb across her parted lips. 'I've never known a woman whose skin was so soft and vulnerable, who changes colour as often as you do.'

Jaime swallowed. 'You said that before,' she told him. 'Or something like it,' she added, striving for an ironic tone. 'It's quite—immature, actually. Like—like these freckles. I've hated them all my life.'

'But I like your freckles,' persisted her tormentor, moving his hand further up her cheek so that he could skim his thumb across her nose. Her face flamed, in spite of all her efforts to the contrary, and he allowed a sound of triumph to escape. 'You see,' he said, 'it makes my role so much easier. I always know when I've struck a nerve.'

'I shouldn't bet on it,' Jaime retorted, giving in to her fears at last, and backing away from him. 'It just means you can embarrass me, that's all. Perhaps what you really enjoy is making fun of me. I doubt if Miss Redding lets you make fun of her.'

She'd spoken thoughtlessly, recklessly, and it was not until his lean, dark features grew sombre that she realised exactly what she had said. 'No,' he said expressionlessly. 'No, you're right. Cat doesn't enjoy my humour either.' He straightened. 'I'm sorry. I was out of line. Forget what I said.'

As if she could.

Jaime closed her eyes for a moment, wishing the last few minutes had never happened. They had been getting along so well. Not—easily, perhaps, but adequately, and although she knew they could never be friends she had felt a certain freedom in his company.

'Do you want to go back?'

His sudden query caught her unawares, and she knew with a terrifying flash of self-knowledge that that was the last thing she wanted to do. 'I—no,' she admitted softly. 'Um—not unless you want to?' And then felt his withering gaze make a nonsense of the question.

'Why would I?' he countered, pulling open one of the deck lockers and taking out rubber flippers and a snorkelling mask. He surveyed her appearance without emotion. 'Do you plan to wear your shirt and shorts to swim?'

Jaime took a breath. 'Of course not.' She crossed her arms and, gripping the hem of the shirt with both hands, tugged it over her head. Then, before she could feel self-conscious, she undid her shorts, stepping out of them just as swiftly, before his knowing eyes could dent her determination. 'I'm ready.'

'So you are.'

His gaze was cool, but disturbing, offering so many inconsistencies. He couldn't really find her attractive, she thought, even if her limbs were slim and modestly shapely. He'd probably known dozens of women like her, but women like Catriona were much rarer. Besides, in his position, he was probably pursued by lots of women. Women with youth, and sophistication, who shared his interests, and were at home in surroundings like these.

'Er—you didn't tell me how much I owe you,' she ventured, desperate to regain his earlier detachment, and Dominic's brows arched quizzically. 'For the suit, I mean,' she tacked on, before he could use her words against her, and comprehension brought a mocking gleam to his eyes.

'You wouldn't consider it a gift, I suppose?' he suggested. And at her defensive stare he went on, 'No, I see you wouldn't. Okay…' He paused, considering. 'I think it was twenty dollars. You can pay me some other time. Now—shall we get on with the lesson?'

Jaime pressed her lips together. 'I'm sure it was more than that.' She touched the silken fabric. 'I can afford it. Your stepmother is paying me quite a lot.'

'And I'm sure you'll earn it,' remarked Dominic drily, stepping down onto the diving platform. 'Okay. D'you want to put these on?'

'These' were a pair of rubber flippers, and she perched rather awkwardly on the rim of the deck to put them on. He really hadn't answered her, and she was no wiser as far as the price of the swimsuit was concerned. She could only hope she'd find the receipt in the bag.

The next few minutes were taken up with him showing her how to adjust the mouthpiece of the snorkel, and the way to use the flippers to propel her through the water. 'You don't need to use your arms,' he explained, and after putting on the other pair of flippers he dived into the water to demonstrate what he meant. 'You're going to be swimming just below the surface,' he added, flicking back his hair with a careless hand. 'The tube that's attached to the mouthpiece will supply you with all the air you need.'

Jaime couldn't wait to get into the water and try it for herself, but she was much less adventurous than Dominic. Sitting on the edge of the platform, she dangled her flippered feet in the water for a moment, and then, taking a nervous breath, she pushed herself off.

The water was wonderful. It swirled about her hot limbs like sun-warmed silk, cooling her, and cleansing her, and giving her a marvellous sense of well-being. And Dominic was right. With the flippers on her feet, she didn't need her arms to swim. Even the most languid kick of her legs gave her propulsion, and she swam about delightedly, testing her strength.

'Don't you need a snorkel, too?' she asked Dominic at last, treading water, having removed the mouthpiece of hers so that she could make herself understood. He'd been waiting patiently while she practised her skills, but now she wondered if he intended to leave her to it.

'I'm okay,' he said, and performed an underwater somersault, as if to reassure her. He grinned. 'I'm used to swimming underwater. Are you ready to swim out to the rocks?'

The next half-hour passed more quickly than Jaime could ever have imagined. With the mask to protect her eyes, she was able to see everything so clearly. The underwater world simply teemed with all kinds of aquatic life and she wanted to protest when Dominic indicated it was time for them to go back to the boat.

It wasn't until she tried to climb back onto the platform that she realised how exhausted she actually was. Although she'd tugged off the mask and thrown it onto the deck, she didn't feel as if she had the strength to pull herself up the ladder. Her legs felt weak and trembly, and even after she'd pulled the flippers off they still wouldn't support her weight. She was obviously not used to so much exercise, and she was glad they hadn't stayed out any longer.

She was wondering what she could do, when Dominic apprehended her dilemma. Pressing the palms of his hands down on the platform, he easily swung himself aboard, and then leant down and lifted her up beside him. 'I guess you overdid it,' he remarked as she lay panting on the deck. 'It's my fault. I should have realised. You're not used to it yet.'

'It wasn't your fault,' declared Jaime firmly, when she got her breath back. She sat up, wringing the water out of her braid, and feeling rather ashamed of herself. 'I didn't want to come back. I thought I could have stayed out much longer. Which just shows what a fool I am.' She grimaced. 'Oh, well—it was fun while it lasted.'

Dominic stood looking down at her. 'You enjoyed it?' he asked, and she seemed to have to look up a long way to reach his face. In the process, her unwilling gaze encountered his worn and dripping denim cut-offs, which clung to his thighs like a second skin, hanging on his hips almost lovingly, exposing the hair that arrowed down to his navel.

'Very much,' she said, her response shortened by her reaction to his leanly muscled body. Oh, God, she thought, she was far too aware of him. If he touched her now, she'd probably melt at his feet.

To her dismay, he did something almost as bad: he came down on his haunches beside her, and now her gaze couldn't help but be drawn to the straining seam between his legs. 'You'd better loosen your hair,' he said, and she grabbed her braid almost protectively. 'It won't dry in that condition. D'you want some help to unfasten it?'

Jaime could hardly speak. 'I—I can manage,' she assured him. 'If—if it's necessary.'

'It is, if you don't want to go back with it dripping all over the car.'

Jaime swallowed. Go back? Her throat dried up. How could she think about going back in this state? She doubted if her limbs would obey her. How was she ever going to face Catriona again?

But that was stupid, she chided herself angrily, tearing at her braid with furious fingers. Just because she had conceived some crazy attraction for Dominic Redding, that was no reason to behave like a schoolgirl. It wasn't as if he shared her feelings; as if he had done anything wrong by spending the afternoon with her. It was all in her mind, and she had to get rid of it. Despite everything else, she knew she should despise him for taking advantage of his father's widow.

The trouble was, it was difficult to see anyone taking advantage of Catriona Redding—unless she wanted them to...

'Is something the matter?' Jaime had been so lost in thought that she had managed to ignore the fact that Dominic was still squatting there, watching her, but now a frown marred his tanned features. 'Did I say something wrong again?' he queried impatiently.

'No—I—I was just thinking about my hair,' replied Jaime untruthfully. 'It's going to take a long time to dry.'

And how long had Catriona Redding been coveting her stepson's hard young body? she wondered, unable to put the wilful thoughts out of her head. What little she knew of him did not lead her to believe that he might have initiated their affair. Though how well did she really know him? Wasn't she deluding herself by imagining she had an insight into his character?

Her gaze flicked over him. What rights did Catriona have so far as he was concerned? she pondered. Did the older woman have the right to touch him, and caress him? To unbutton those tight denims, and peel them down over his thighs, and—?

'There's a hairdryer below deck.' Dominic's voice interrupted her wild abstraction. It seemed to come from a distance, but she knew it was her own mind that was endeavouring to keep him at arm's length. 'You can even take a shower, if you'd like to get the salt off your skin,' he added. 'I promise not to take advantage of you again.'

'Again?'

Jaime stared at him blankly, her hair loose now, and spreading like a wet cape about her shoulders. Its dark red colour had been deepened by the soaking it had received, but where the sun caught its length strands of gold gleamed with a fiery light.

'Yes, again,' said Dominic, almost absently, his whole attention caught and held by the unknowingly sensual picture she presented. He moved, dropping down onto one knee to keep his balance, and regarded her with a disturbingly sensuous gaze. 'What a waste,' he breathed, grasping a handful of her hair and winding it about his fingers. 'You should always wear your hair like this.'

She should have pulled away. She would have pulled away, she told herself later, if her senses hadn't still been inflamed by the sexual images she had evoked. As it was, she seemed to have no will to stop him. She let him take her hair in his hand; she let him smooth the damp strands between his finger and thumb; she let him carry its gleaming bounty to his lips.

She sat there, almost numb with anticipation, as he rubbed her hair against his mouth. She would never have believed that such a simple act could create such a quivering deep inside her, but it did. The touch of his lips caused such a storm of sensation that she almost moaned out loud, and she could tell from the lazy sexuality in his eyes that he knew exactly how she felt.

'It's beautiful,' he said huskily, and Jaime forced her brain to work.

'It's wet,' she said, swallowing convulsively.

'Where—where is this hairdryer you were talking about?'

'It's in one of the cabins,' he replied, making no attempt to move away from her. 'There's no hurry, is there? It's barely five o'clock.'

'Five o'clock!'

Jaime was horrified. At this rate, she wouldn't get back until after six. She dreaded to think what she was going to tell Catriona. Did he expect her to tell his stepmother the truth?

'Don't look like that.' To her relief his voice had hardened somewhat, and she hoped that meant he was going to let her go. 'We haven't done anything wrong,' he added, almost mirroring the thoughts she had had earlier. His eyes darkened. 'Though I have to admit I'm tempted. Very tempted.'

'I don't think so.'

Jaime knew she had to take the initiative here, and, infusing a note of irony into her voice, she attempted to extricate herself from his grasp. But when she put up her hand to pull her hair away his hand closed about her wrist, and, far from freeing herself, she found herself more securely trapped than ever.

'Mr Redding—'

'For God's sake, stop calling me that,' he growled irritably, and she heaved a nervous sigh.

'Dominic, then,' she placated him. 'Dominic, please—let go of me. I've got to go and dry my hair.'

'And take this off?' he asked, his free hand skimming the strapless rim of the bodice of her swimsuit. His finger inserted itself into the elasticated fabric. 'Let me help you.' His eyes imprisoned hers. 'It feels—tight.'

It was. Mainly because his sensual words and the frankly carnal expression in his eyes were causing her breasts to swell and harden. She could feel her nipples, button-hard against the wet silk, obviously visible, and giving the lie to any denial she might make.

'Dominic—'

Her lips trembled, the quivering in her legs spreading up into her stomach. Oh, God, she thought, she wanted him to touch her. She could think of nothing more desirable than to feel his hands against her hot skin.

'Jaime,' he said, matching her use of his name, but without the doubts she had exhibited. His hand slid from her wrist to her shoulder, and from there to the vulnerable nape of her neck. 'Jaime,' he said again, his fingers curving to the shape of her, and covered her protesting mouth with his...

CHAPTER EIGHT

'BY THE way, Cat, I'm leaving tomorrow.'

Dominic had his back to the room as he spoke, his attention apparently absorbed in the task of pouring whisky from the decanter into his glass. It meant Catriona couldn't see his expression as he said the words—and that he didn't have to face her predictable response.

'Leaving!' Catriona's sudden intake of breath was sufficiently charged to give him some indication of her feelings. There was a pregnant pause before she asked, 'When did you decide this?'

About five minutes after I gave in to the urge to kiss Jaime Harris, thought Dominic grimly. But, 'This afternoon,' he answered, lifting his glass and turning to look at her. 'You knew I was planning to go back this week.'

'But not on Friday!' protested Catriona, her long, scarlet-tipped fingers beating a tattoo against the arm of her chair. She took another frustrated breath, uncrossing and recrossing her legs with obvious irritation. 'Why not go back on Monday? Then we can have the weekend together.'

Dominic propped his hip against the polished cabinet behind him, and raised his glass to his lips. 'Can't be done,' he stated evenly, after swallowing a mouthful of the single malt. 'For one thing, I need the weekend to read my mail, and catch up on what's been happening, and for another I have a meeting with Thomas Aitken's agent on Monday morning.'

'Thomas Aitken?' Catriona was impressed, and for a moment she savoured the prospect of seeing her books

90

being sold alongside the Pulitzer-winning author's. Then, remembering her grievance, she fixed Dominic with a resentful stare. 'You didn't tell me this meeting had been arranged.'

'Because I didn't know myself until earlier this evening,' retorted Dominic honestly, though he didn't add that the timing of the meeting had been at his request. 'I know for a fact that Dyson has already sent the manuscript to several publishers, but Aitken promised my father he'd give us first refusal this time.'

'So long as you come up with a competitive bid,' said Catriona cynically, considering the outcome, and Dominic was glad to discuss his expectations, if it avoided a more personal discord.

'Oh, sure. We don't expect him to do us any favours in that department,' he agreed. 'But it was Dad who pulled a few strings and got him his first job in journalism, and he hasn't forgotten. Aitken didn't start out with the *New York Times,* you know.'

'I know.' Catriona sipped at her white wine, which was the only alcohol she ever touched. 'All the same, I do think you could have left it to Paul Rivers. This is only a preliminary meeting, isn't it? It's unlikely that any decisions will be made.'

'Maybe.' But Dominic was grateful for the excuse. 'In any case, I've wasted enough time.'

Catriona's eyes sparkled, but not with anticipation. 'Is that what you think?' she demanded. 'That coming here, spending these few days with me, has just been a waste of time?'

'I didn't say that.' Dominic controlled the urge to swear. 'But you have to admit I've recovered. There's no real reason for me to hang about here any longer.'

'You don't consider my feelings might constitute a reason?' she enquired resentfully. 'Honestly, Dom, I sometimes wonder how much more of this I can take. You don't seem to care that you're hurting me when you make these pronouncements. It never even occurs to you that once you're gone I'm completely alone.'

Dominic suppressed a weary groan. 'You're not alone.'

'Aren't I?'

'No.' He sighed. 'You've got friends here. Not to mention Samuel and Sophie. And—' he paused '—there's Miss Harris, of course.'

'Her!'

Catriona was scathing, and Dominic felt an unfamiliar twinge of indigestion in his gut. Dammit, she had no right to dismiss Jaime as if she were of no importance. She was a human being, wasn't she? And one who appeared to care more for Catriona's good opinion than she should.

He scowled down at his drink, wishing he had never brought her name into this. Catriona was sure to wonder later—if not now—why he should have instantly thought of her. He was only grateful he had remembered to use her surname. Her first name came far too easily to his lips.

'You think I should make a friend of her, do you?'

Catriona was in no mood to miss any hint of complicity and Dominic realised he had made a big mistake. Jaime provided exactly the kind of scapegoat Catriona needed, and he steeled himself to face another tirade.

'I just think you exaggerate your isolation,' he replied carefully. 'And it's not as if you're confined to the islands. Dad's apartment is always available. I'm sure Jennings would welcome the opportunity to have something to do.'

'And if I came to New York Miss Harris would come too; is that what you think?'

Catriona was incensed now, and Dominic knew an overwhelming sense of déjà vu. This wasn't the first time they had had this kind of argument, and it didn't help to know that this time he was guilty as charged.

'I don't give a—damn whether you bring Miss Harris or not,' he declared at last, restraining his use of epithets at the last minute. In fact, he thought, he'd like it a whole lot better if she left Jaime in Bermuda. Perhaps then he'd be able to understand what was going on.

He emptied his glass, and turned away to refill it. God, he thought savagely, whatever had possessed him to lay a hand on the other woman? It wasn't as if she was beautiful, or irresistible—or flirtatious, as Kristin had been. He must have been mad to think of having sex with her, to lose his head so completely he'd almost succumbed.

And yet, at the time, it had seemed perfectly natural. Jaime had sat there, on the deck of the *Nightwing*, gazing up at him so candidly, she had seemed to epitomise temptation in all its forms. She hadn't been aware of it, but he'd felt the tremor that had gone through her body when he'd touched her. She'd undressed him with her eyes, and he'd been hooked.

More than hooked, he admitted, feeling the involuntary stirring of his body. No other woman had ever been able to turn him on with just a look. He'd always considered himself reasonably in control of his emotions. Even his feelings for Catriona had always been securely regulated by his mind.

'I just find your attitude so—so confusing, darling.' While he had been struggling to contain his emotions, Catriona had evidently decided to forgive him, and her voice came from right behind him. Lifting the hem of his dark silk jacket, she slid her arms about his waist and pressed herself intimately against him. 'I don't want us to quarrel,' she whispered. 'Particularly not if you're going away tomorrow.'

Dominic closed his eyes against the feeling of weariness that washed over him at that moment. He could feel the sinuous length of her against him, from the small breasts that pressed against his jacket to the leg that she kicked free of her slit skirt and insinuated between both of his.

But at least it achieved something, he reflected wryly as his erection subsided. When her greedy fingers probed the button at his waist, he had no fear of her succeeding in what she craved. Much as he might regret the knowledge, tonight Catriona's caresses were just an irritation. His mind was miles from here, on the yacht in Spiny Bay...

Jaime's lips had been so much softer than he had anticipated. And the kiss—which had never been intended to be taken seriously—had somehow got away from him. Instead of drawing back after the half-teasing salutation he'd initiated, the touch of her mouth had caused an entirely unexpected reaction, and he'd found himself sinking into her, deepening and lengthening the kiss, until his lungs had been burning and desperate for air.

But even then he hadn't let go of her. He seemed to remember she'd made some instinctive sound of protest when he'd first bent towards her, but her objection had been a trifling thing at best. She'd seemed as overwhelmed by the heat that enveloped them as he was, and she certainly hadn't stopped him when he'd pushed his tongue between her teeth...

'Dom! Dom, are you listening to me?'

With a start, he realised Catriona was speaking to him, and, suppressing the impatience that her interruption inspired, he turned to face her. In so doing, he also dislodged her clinging embrace, though her fingers fastened on his lapels with equal determination.

'You weren't listening, were you?' she accused him painfully. 'Oh, Dom—' Her eyes filled with tears. 'What have I said? What have I done to make you treat me like this? I don't know what's happening to us.'

Nor did he. But...

'Nothing's happening to us,' he told her firmly, his hands closing about her slim wrists with gentle conviction. 'Now, what were you saying? Something about us not quarrelling tonight?'

Catriona sniffed. 'That's all very well,' she said, her thumbs stroking the underside of his jaw, 'but you know I can't live in New York. I can't work there. You know that.'

Dominic despised himself for the relief he felt at her admission. Much as he wished he could rekindle the feelings that being with her had always aroused in him, right now his emotions felt as if they were frozen. He still wanted to marry Catriona. That went without saying. But he was no longer in any doubt that he needed more time.

But time for what? a small voice inside him goaded. Time to sow a few wild oats, perhaps; time to satisfy his lust? The hours he'd spent with Jaime had left him feeling restless. Was he one of those pathetic bastards who only wanted what he couldn't have?

The memories swept over him again, memories of tangling his hands in Jaime's long hair, of cupping her head between his hands, and holding her still while he plundered her mouth. He hadn't wanted to let her go, he admitted ruefully. He'd wanted to make love with her, to lay her back on the sun-warmed deck and bury his aching body in her yielding flesh...

He hadn't done it, of course. Although he might have found the idea of spending the next few hours discovering the many delights of her unexpectedly responsive body appealing, he had still retained an atom of common sense. Dear God, he had barely exchanged a few words with Kristin and Catriona had sent her packing. How would she have reacted if she had seen him with Jaime? It didn't bear thinking about.

But it had been sweet; so sweet. He didn't know whether Jaime would have let him go all the way, but there was no denying that when he'd thrust his tongue into her mouth she'd seemed incapable of resisting him.

She'd clutched at his neck with those hot little hands that had felt like fire against his skin, gripping his hair to pull herself closer and creating a matching fire in his loins.

He hadn't been thinking very sensibly then, he admitted. Peeling her swimsuit down to her waist, so that her plump breasts had surged against his chest, had been madness of the first order. Her nipples had played havoc with his reeling senses, but it hadn't been until he had fastened his teeth about one plum-coloured areola that the realisation of what he was doing had knocked him cold.

Even then, it had been painful to draw back. With the blood pounding thickly through his veins, and every nerve in his body straining towards a fulfilment he hadn't received, it had been almost agony to drag himself away. It had only been telling himself that it was just sex he was starved of that had eventually enabled him to get things into perspective. It wasn't Jaime he wanted, he'd told himself; it was a woman. Which was why he had decided to go back to New York.

Of course, it had been an embarrassing journey back to the marina.

Whatever contempt he might feel for himself as a man, he was not used to making a fool of any woman, and particularly not someone who seemed as reserved— and innocent—as Jaime. Leaving her there on the deck, propelling himself forward, to enable her to slip down into the cabin and dress herself, had been the hardest thing he'd ever done, and he'd hardly been surprised when she'd avoided speaking to him for the rest of the trip.

Luckily the wind had been favourable, and they'd dropped anchor in Webb's Cove within forty minutes. Dominic had secured the hatches while Jaime climbed into the dinghy, and then he'd started the outboard motor and guided the small craft back to the quay.

It hadn't been until he'd started towards the car that she'd found her voice.

'I shan't be going back with you,' she'd said, her face flaming as he'd turned to look at her. He'd seen that she had found the hairdryer and dried her hair and it was now screwed back into the chunky plait she usually wore. There had been no trace then of the sensuous woman he had kissed in Spiny Bay; no trace of any emotion but cold contempt. 'I'll ask Mr Erskine to call me a taxi.' She'd paused then and given him a scathing look. 'I don't want Miss Redding to get the wrong idea.'

'Could she?'

He remembered his response now with a trace of shame. He shouldn't have said anything. What had happened between them had been his fault, yet by using those sardonic words he had shifted half the blame onto her. He hadn't been surprised when she'd turned away in disgust. He disgusted himself sometimes. Like now; making excuses for going away.

'So, when will you be coming back?' Catriona pressed him, her parted lips red and avid, her hungry gaze fixed on his lean mouth. 'At least give me something to look forward to. I want us to be married before Christmas.'

Christmas!

Dominic's mouth dried. On the fifteenth of December, it would be exactly eighteen months since his father died. It should be long enough for anyone. And Catriona would be forty-five by then.

'All right,' he conceded, assuring himself that whatever sickness he was suffering would be gone by then. For God's sake, this was the woman he'd destroyed his marriage for, wasn't it? He knew at least half a dozen other men who would do murder to be in his shoes.

'You mean it? We can get married before Christmas?'

Clearly, she had not been expecting him to agree, but Dominic ignored the mocking demon at his elbow. 'Why not?' he said, with determined enthusiasm. 'We could make it a double celebration.' And at her blank expression he added, 'It's your birthday at the end of November, isn't it?'

Catriona's face cleared. 'Oh. Oh, of course,' she said, her hands groping for his neck, twining in the hair at his nape. She pulled his face towards hers. 'Oh, Dom, you've made me so happy. I might even come to New York in a few weeks. After all, we have to buy a ring.'

Dominic left on the morning flight.

Despite her promise to see him off, Catriona had not appeared by the time he left the house. Perhaps she'd thought he might go to her apartments to say his goodbyes, but Dominic had been grateful for the reprieve. It had been hard enough getting up with the hangover he'd deliberately brought on himself by drinking too much the night before. There was no way he was going down that road again, not when he didn't have the excuse of being drunk to save him.

He hadn't seen Jaime since the previous afternoon. He assumed she'd arrived home by taxi. He didn't honestly know what had happened to her. After their bitter exchange on the jetty, he had got into the four-by-four and driven away. Mainly because he had been in such a foul mood with himself, he freely admitted. But also because he was angry with her, for the unholy mess she was making of his life.

Yet it wasn't her fault, he assured himself, staring down at the islands spread out below him as the big jet banked before levelling out on its flight path to JFK. He'd been restless before Jaime Harris had taken up her position as Catriona's assistant, he decided. She had just been the catalyst who had forced him to take a closer look at his life.

And, whether he chose to pacify Catriona or not, he needed a woman in his bed. He stretched his legs out in front of him as an unwilling image of Jaime caused a sudden constriction of his trousers. And that was all it was, he berated himself: sexual deprivation. He'd been celibate for far too long.

God knew, it was easy enough to get laid in his home city. Apart from all the free talent around, there were escort agencies and computer dating agencies wall-to-wall. In the past, he'd had no difficulty in accommodating his needs, as and when the need had struck him. For a man who wanted no commitment, New York was definitely the place.

But that evening he found himself switching channels in the comfortable living room of his apartment. Instead of picking up the phone and dialling for company, he'd dialled for a take-out pizza instead. Contrary to everything he'd told himself since that afternoon on the yacht, he hadn't been able to get Jaime out of his mind.

Which was crazy! For God's sake, he thought, he was too old to become infatuated with someone else. He was just going through a minor crisis, brought on by his sense of loyalty to his father. It would pass, and he'd remember this evening with contempt.

CHAPTER NINE

'HAVE you finished those notes yet?'

Catriona emerged from her study as Jaime was typing the last page, and she finished the sentence she had been transcribing before looking at her employer.

'I've got half a page still to do,' she said, feeling the familiar twinge of anxiety she always felt in Catriona's presence. It was all very well telling herself that so far as Catriona was concerned she was an efficient typist and little else. That didn't alter the fact that deep down she felt a traitor, even if the reasons for that emotion were more imagined than real.

'Hmm.' Catriona came to look over her shoulder, enveloping her in a cloud of expensive perfume. 'You've made a mistake there: that should read gauge, not guess.'

Jaime drew a breath. 'I think you'll find you've got guess in your notes,' she declared politely, aware that if she changed it to gauge now she could still be accused of being wrong. 'There it is—you say Malcolm tried to guess the contents. Would you like me to change it to gauge anyway?'

Catriona's mouth thinned. 'You're very precise, aren't you?' she remarked crisply. 'Almost too precise—or is that a contradiction in terms? Tell me, do you ever make a mistake, Miss Harris? Or are you one of those people who never get things wrong?'

Jaime moistened her lips. 'I get things wrong, Miss Redding.'

'Do you?' Catriona positioned herself so that Jaime was forced to look at her. 'What?'

'What do I get wrong?'

'That's what I asked.'

Jaime swallowed, trying desperately to think of something impersonal to say. 'Um—I often make mistakes in—in my typing. I just correct them before you see the finished draft.'

Catriona's mouth drew in, but instead of being satisfied with Jaime's answer and going back into her study, as her assistant had hoped, she draped one silk-clad thigh over the corner of the desk and regarded her enquiringly. 'I wasn't just talking about your work,' she declared, her lips tightening. 'Well, perhaps I was to begin with. You look so—so composed most of the time. Demure, almost. You make me curious, Miss Harris. Have you ever made a mistake about a man?'

Jaime managed not to catch her breath. 'I— Have you?' she countered, playing for time, and Catriona gave a scornful laugh before picking up a paperclip from the desk.

'Of course,' she replied at last, after bending the paperclip out of all recognition. And as Jaime stiffened she continued, 'I should never have married Larry. He was far too old for me, but I'm afraid I was overwhelmed by his wealth and influence. In any event, as soon as I met Dom, I knew I'd made a terrible mistake.'

'But Dominic was only sixteen!' Jaime protested, before she had considered her words. And then, to cover herself, she added, 'Um—I believe that's what Samuel told me. Isn't that right?'

Catriona's eyes had narrowed. 'Samuel told you that?'

'Well, it might have been Sophie,' murmured Jaime uncomfortably, aware that she was digging a hole for herself, and unable to do anything about it. She could only hope to distract Catriona from asking the servants. 'I'm afraid I asked how long you and Mr Redding had been married.'

'Did you indeed?' Catriona frowned. 'And why would that interest you?'

'I—wondered how long you had been writing,' declared Jaime, desperate to divert the course of this conversation. 'In any case, I'm sure you and Mr Redding were very happy together.'

'Larry was happy, that's true,' said Catriona, shrugging her shoulders. 'And I always gave him credit for directing my style of writing, although I suspect he knew I'd have made it anyway.'

Jaime moistened her dry lips. 'He didn't help you?'

'Heavens, no.' Whatever doubts she might have had about her writing in the past, Catriona was supremely confident now. 'Oh, I'm not denying that Goldman and Redding were responsible for my first book getting published, but I like to think that would have happened with or without their participation.'

'I see.'

'I've also spent the last twenty years or so trying to forgive Larry for refusing to publish my detective novels,' she continued. 'You didn't know about them, did you? Oh, yes. I wrote three cosy whodunits before I turned my talents to historical fiction.'

'Really?' Jaime swallowed.

'Yes, really.' Catriona had warmed to her theme. 'I sometimes wonder if I'd have had more recognition if I'd continued writing detective stories. Historical romance unfortunately doesn't have the kudos that crime fiction has always had.'

'I see.' Jaime saw her chance and took it. 'So how long were you writing before you—before you met your—your husband?'

'Not long.' Catriona's mouth drew in, as if the memories Jaime's words had evoked were not to her liking. 'I like to think my life began when I first went to New York. Until then, well, it was humdrum, to say the least.'

Jaime licked her lips nervously. 'Um—what did you do?'

'What did I do?' Catriona frowned. 'You mean, what was my occupation?'

Jaime hadn't meant that exactly, but she could hardly elaborate. 'Well, yes,' she said instead, hoping to gain some knowledge of Catriona's movements before she'd left England. 'Did—er—did you live in London?'

Catriona hesitated, as if weighing her words before replying. 'London?' she queried, as if the name were unfamiliar to her. 'I—no. No, I lived in Devon. I had a couple of interviews in London, but like you I wanted to work in more congenial surroundings.'

Jaime's nostrils flared. She longed to confront her. She longed to say that, far from despising the busy streets, it was because of her that they had lived in Chiswick. Her father would have much preferred the country. Unfortunately by the time his wife abandoned him he was too dispirited to throw up his job and start again somewhere else.

'So—what did you do?' she asked now, pushing her luck, but needing the consolation of knowing she hadn't just given in. She was betraying everything her father stood for by being here, but she hoped he'd have understood her need to find out the truth.

Catriona sighed. 'Why do you want to know?' she asked, without answering her. Her eyes narrowed. 'You're not one of those undercover journalists, are you, looking for the secrets in my past?'

Jaime took a breath. 'Why?' she asked. 'Do you have any?' And then, because that was rather too dangerous, she said, 'No. I'm curious, that's all. I—I'm sure any of your readers would be interested in knowing what encouraged you to take up writing in the first place.'

'Hmm.' Catriona didn't sound altogether convinced, but her ego was such that she was prepared to overlook her suspicions in favour of the story that was evidently well rehearsed. 'As a matter of fact, I worked as a nanny,' she said, sliding gracefully off the desk. 'And now I think I must get some work done. I can't stand here chatting all day.'

'In Devon?' asked Jaime insistently, wanting to be sure that that was what Catriona had said, and the other woman eyed her with real impatience now. 'Where you worked as a nanny,' she added, although the idea that Catriona had done that filled her with an aching regret. To think she had abandoned her own baby, to look after someone else's, was more than painful. It was unjust.

'For someone who professes to be a fan of mine, you're not very knowledgeable,' Catriona remarked tersely now. 'Haven't you ever read the bio on the jackets of my books?'

Jaime had never read that!

'It's—it's different, hearing it from you,' she managed weakly. Then, infusing a note of admiration into her voice, she said, 'I thought you must have lived abroad. You say very little about your early life.'

'That's because I didn't have a very exciting life before I met Larry,' declared Catriona indifferently. 'And I was only twenty-five when I went to New York. If you're wondering where I lived when I was a child, that's different. As a matter of fact, my parents lived in the north of England, and I lived there too, until—until—'

'Until?' Jaime prompted, holding her breath.

'Until I moved south, of course,' answered Catriona disappointingly. She moved towards her study door. 'If that's all, I must get on.'

Jaime wanted to stop her. She wanted to ask her why, if she'd lived in the north of England all her life, she'd moved to Devon, of all places. It wasn't that there was anything wrong with Devon. Goodness knew, Jaime and her father had spent a couple of holidays at Torquay. But it wasn't the destination most young people chose. But then Jaime knew that Catriona's real reason for moving south—to London, in fact—had been that she'd met and married Jaime's father.

If there had been any doubt in her mind before this, it was all banished now. Catriona was Cathryn Michaels—or she had been, before she'd met and married Lawrence Redding twenty years ago. Had she got a divorce? That was something else Jaime needed to know. If she hadn't, her marriage to Dominic's father was just a sham.

To her relief, Catriona spent the remainder of the day in her study, and Jaime wasn't given the chance to ask any more questions. Despite a few awkward moments, she was aware that she had got off rather easily, but she suspected her employer wouldn't forget how curious she had been.

Supper that evening consisted of ravioli stuffed with ricotta cheese, and sea bass served with a lobster sauce. The food at the villa was always delicious, and Jaime reflected that if she wasn't careful she'd start putting on weight. It had not been a problem in London. Looking after her father in the final months of his illness had seen to that. And besides, she was used to looking after herself. Dashing into supermarkets, on her way home from work, was a sure-fire way of ensuring she stayed slim.

For the first time, after Samuel had taken away her tray and the door was securely locked, Jaime pulled her suitcase out of the closet, and extracted the wallet that she had pushed into the side pocket. The wallet contained all the official documents and papers she had found in the strongbox, after her father's death. The documents and papers that had alerted her to her mother's identity, and the secret Robert Michaels had been guarding for so long.

Because she had been so young when her mother disappeared, she could never actually remember what it had been like to have a real mother. Besides, her grandmother—her father's mother—had always been there to fill the role her mother should have played. She'd been much older, of course, and they hadn't had a lot in common, but Jaime had loved her very much.

By the time old Mrs Michaels died, Jaime had been a teenager, and well able to take care of herself. In actual fact, she was already looking after herself and her father, choosing to attend a London university after she'd passed her exams so that she could continue to live at home.

So far as she knew, her father had never thought of getting married again, and conversations she had instigated about her mother had tended to end unsatisfactorily at best. He had always maintained that he had not heard from her mother again, and she believed him. But he'd never admitted that he knew where she was and what she was doing now.

That was why the papers Jaime had found after his death had given her such a shock. At first, she hadn't been able to understand why her father should have collected so many clippings about a woman writer she hardly knew. But then she'd found her parents' photograph, and put two and two together. Despite the flattering pictures on the back of Catriona Redding's books, the resemblance had been too obvious to miss.

She knew now that her father must have expected her to find the information after he was dead, but she had no idea what he had expected her to do with it. Perhaps he'd hoped she'd ignore it. It was certain that her mother had shown no interest in her for almost thirty years. But hope had sprung eternal, and Jaime had known she had to find out what her mother was really like.

The opportunity to apply for this job had come some three months later, while Jaime was still trying to pluck up the courage to contact her mother. She had jumped at the chance to meet Cathryn Michaels—Catriona Redding—in person, with the added bonus of her not knowing who she was.

Smoothing the clipping that announced the publication of her mother's first book with nervous fingers, Jaime felt a not unfamiliar twinge of apprehension. She had had no idea when she'd applied for this position that so many complications could ensue. But then, she had had no idea that Catriona was such a vain woman, or that she might be in the throes of conducting an affair with her late husband's son.

Dominic.

Jaime took a deep breath. For the past couple of days, ever since Catriona had told her that Dominic had gone back to New York, in actual fact, Jaime had succeeded in keeping any thoughts of her employer's stepson safely at the back of her mind. She had no reason to think about him, she told herself; no reason at all to relive those moments on the yacht. Because of his relationship with his stepmother, he had had no right to play games with her emotions, particularly as they both knew how vindictive Catriona could be. As far as Dominic was concerned, she had applied for this job and she needed to keep it. His behaviour could have put her position in jeopardy, and she told herself she despised him for behaving so badly.

Her own feelings notwithstanding, she doubted that anything about that afternoon had bothered him. His approach had been far too practised, far too experienced. He had always been in control of his feelings, whereas she had been lost from the start. No wonder Catriona guarded him so jealously, she thought bitterly. He must do wonders for her ego.

She shivered. It wasn't wise to think about Dominic. Even now, she could feel the caressing touch of his hands on her hot skin, the weakness as he'd suckled on her breasts. Almost involuntarily, her hands moved to soothe the aching need her thoughts had aroused inside her, feeling her thrusting nipples beneath her palms.

It wouldn't do.

Blinking back the tears that were suddenly hot behind

her eyes, Jaime grasped the clippings and thrust them back into the wallet. Her birth certificate and the telling marriage certificate followed, together with the faded photograph, which had been taken on her parents' wedding day. Her lips twisted at the sight of the simple snapshot, and she briefly held her parents' image in her hand. The picture was a close-up, taken outside the small church where they had been married, and their hands were clasped at chest height, as if to show off their rings to the camera. She sighed. There was no way she could show the revealing picture to Dominic. It was not her place to tell him what her mother had done.

So what was she going to do? It was obvious that Cathryn/Catriona had invented a whole new identity for herself when she'd left Robert Michaels, and Jaime didn't have the stomach to destroy it. And yet... She hesitated as the suspicion that her mother had never got a divorce resurrected itself. Surely if her father had been served with divorce papers they too would have been in the wallet, or in the box in which she'd found it. His insurances had been there, and the deeds of the house in Chiswick. Indeed the strongbox had contained everything of value he had possessed.

But nothing about the divorce, even though he had obviously known her mother had married again. Still, as he'd never attempted to contact his ex-wife, how could she expect him to have made an issue of this?

Jaime sighed again. There was a period of about five years unaccounted for, by her reckoning. Was that when Cathryn had lived in Devon as Catriona had said? She had probably changed her first name then, too, although she had apparently used her maiden surname. Dominic's casual remark about her earlier novels had explained a lot.

Jaime pushed the wallet back into the suitcase and closed the closet door. Then, with the damning evidence safely out of sight again, she emptied the small carafe of wine Samuel had brought her into her glass, and stepped out onto the verandah.

What was she going to do?

What she should do was simple enough, she acknowledged wryly. Having come here, having achieved her objective by meeting and getting to know Catriona Redding without revealing her own identity, she should leave. It was the most sensible course of action, after all, and she doubted Catriona would object. For all she could find no fault with her work, Jaime had the feeling that Catriona didn't really like her. But whether that was because Dominic had shown some interest in her or for some other unknown reason she couldn't be sure.

Whatever, Jaime sensed that testing those waters might prove painful. For all she might tell herself that she didn't care what Cathryn—Catriona—thought of her, it wasn't true. She wished she could find it in her heart to forgive her but she'd discovered her own skin was much thinner than she'd thought.

CHAPTER TEN

JAIME was still undecided as to what her next course of action should be when Catriona came into her office the next morning, and announced that she was going to New York to see Dominic.

'He's been pestering me to join him ever since he left,' she declared smugly. 'He's such a persuasive boy. How could I refuse?'

How indeed? thought Jaime painfully, not at all sure why Catriona's words should hurt. For heaven's sake, *she* hadn't taken his advances seriously. For all she'd made such a fool of herself, she'd never been in any doubt that she had just been a momentary diversion.

Now, moistening lips that were dry in spite of the admonition she had made to herself, she lifted her head. 'Oh?' she managed politely. 'Um—when are you leaving?'

'Tomorrow,' said Catriona firmly. 'Perhaps you'd get on to the airline and book me on the morning flight. I'll ring Dominic and tell him when to expect me. He'll probably insist on meeting me, so don't bother to arrange for a limousine to meet me at the airport.'

'Very well, Miss Redding.' Jaime was aware she was finding it harder and harder to use the woman's professional name. Despite the instinct that warned her to do nothing about it, the temptation to tell her mother who she was wasn't totally suppressed. 'Would you like me to come with you?'

Now why had she asked that?

'That won't be necessary.' There was no hesitation in Catriona's voice, and despite the relief she should have been feeling Jaime felt a certain sense of ignominy at the words. Catriona's lips curved in anticipation. 'I shan't need a secretary while I'm staying with Dominic,' she added. 'This isn't a business trip, Miss Harris. I intend to have fun.'

'I see.'

Whether Catriona sensed a note of censure in her response Jaime couldn't be sure, but her next words were in the nature of a reproof. 'I am entitled to take a holiday when I feel like it, Miss Harris. Besides—' she flicked a careless nail across the pages of manuscript on Jaime's desk '—I've reached something of an impasse. I need a little—stimulation—to—to sharpen my sexual edge, so to speak.'

To Jaime's relief, Catriona disappeared into her study after this remark, probably to make the call to her stepson, Jaime surmised. At least she wouldn't be there, looking over their shoulders, she thought with determined firmness. And Dominic wouldn't need to console himself with her because his sexual demands weren't being met.

Nevertheless, Jaime did feel a little at a loose end after Catriona had departed the following morning. Samuel had been seconded to drive her to the airport, and although Jaime would have willingly undertaken the task she hadn't been asked. She would have enjoyed the journey, she reflected ruefully. She'd had little interest in her surroundings when she'd arrived. And the airport was near St George's, which was at the other end of the island altogether, as Dominic had said.

Still, with Catriona expected back in three or four days—she couldn't be more definite than that, she'd told her secretary coyly—Jaime had things to do to keep her occupied. There was the daily influx of mail to open, autographed pictures to be despatched to adoring fans, and several pages of Catriona's notes to be transcribed. In addition to which her employer had suggested that she might take the opportunity to reorganise the files. Catriona kept every letter that was sent to her, and as they'd become hopelessly muddled an alphabetical index was required.

Jaime spent the morning transcribing the notes, and then ate a solitary lunch in the morning room. She would have preferred it if Sophie had suggested that she share hers and Samuel's lunch in the kitchen, but the house-keeper wasn't the kind of person to invite that kind of intimacy.

And, although the lunches she had shared with Catriona hadn't always been enjoyable occasions, Jaime found she missed her. It was better to have to listen to her employer congratulating herself on how hard she worked, and how ungrateful people were not to appreciate it, than to have no one to listen to at all. At present, her own thoughts were so chaotic, she'd have welcomed any diversion.

When the meal was over, she returned to her desk, but the swaying palms beyond her window were an ir-resistible temptation. Why shouldn't she go for a walk? she thought. It wasn't as if she had any timetable to keep to. It was hot, of course, but perhaps she could find some shade. It would be so pleasant to get away from the house.

She sped along the walkway to her suite of rooms, and quickly changed out of the blouse and skirt she had worn to work in. A pair of shorts in lime-green cotton with a matching vest took their place, and she secured her braid in a knot on top of her head.

Viewing her appearance in the long mirrors, she had to admit she looked better than she'd done on her arrival. Her skin had lost its paleness, and had taken on a golden tinge. Even the hated freckles seemed less conspicuous.

It was the way she was dressed, she decided, realising the vest and shorts were much more appealing than any-thing she might have worn in England. She sighed, suddenly remembering the attractive swimsuit Dominic had bought her, and which was presently stuffed away at the bottom of her drawer. Perhaps she should pay more attention to her appearance, she reflected, with sudden doubt. At home, it was true, she was more inclined to dress like one of her own students than their tutor.

And, looking at her reflection now, she could see that she did have certain good points. Her eyes were widespaced and candid, and her lashes were of a reasonable length. The fact that they were gold-tipped rather spoilt the image, she thought. A vain woman would have darkened them with mascara.

She also had slim limbs. Her body might be more generous than she would have liked, but her arms and legs were not unshapely. What was certain, she thought ironically, was that she did not take after her mother. Compared to Catriona's striking beauty, she was a pale shadow.

The sand was hot, but the breeze off the ocean was appealing. Jaime had taken the precaution of applying a sunscreen to her bare arms and legs before she'd left the house, so she didn't think she was in any danger of getting burned. She kept her neck cool by scooping up handfuls of the cool salt water to moisten it, and her spirits lifted in spite of her mood.

She still hadn't decided what she was going to do when Catriona got back from New York. Her probationary two weeks would be up in a couple of days, and although she might be invited to stay longer what would be the point? It was true she had no commitments at the university until the start of the autumn term, but that was no real excuse for hanging on.

She had kicked off her sandals as soon as she'd stepped onto the beach, and now she paddled along the shoreline looking for crabs. The damp sand slid away between her toes, and several of the tiny sand crabs were exposed. But they scuttled away to bury themselves again, hiding their heads in the sand—much as she was doing, she reflected wryly.

It was a shame to turn back, but eventually she had to, aware that the incoming tide could trap her in one of the rocky coves. These cliffs had no caves, just a wild and craggy beauty, and in any case there was no escape from the anguish of her thoughts.

The house seemed strangely silent when she got back, but she knew it was only her imagination. It wasn't as if Catriona had filled the house with guests when she was at home, and it was only the knowledge that both her mother and Dominic were in New York that made the place feel so absurdly empty.

The thought of going to her own suite of rooms was not appealing so, as Catriona was away and unable to be disturbed, Jaime decided to start on the files. It was better to keep occupied, she'd found, and it was going to be a long job.

A *very* long job, she amended some time later, after discovering that many of the letters were almost impossible to read. In some cases it was the handwriting, but in others the ink had faded, and she had to use all her initiative to work out who had sent them.

She was hot, too. Because the air-conditioning had felt chilly on her hot flesh when she'd first come into Catriona's study, she'd turned it off, and now she was reaping the rewards of her mistake. Getting up from Catriona's desk, she went to turn it on again, and as she did so she noticed the key that was lying on the floor behind the cabinet.

She picked it up, and turned it over in her hand. It was just an ordinary key, the kind that fitted a small cupboard, or a desk. A desk-drawer, surmised Jaime thoughtfully, guessing Catriona had dropped it on her way out. Which meant she must have intended to take it with her. But what could she possibly need to keep locked up in the house?

Jaime frowned, her intention to turn on the air-conditioner forgotten as she stared down at the small gold key in her hand. Knowing the woman as she did, she couldn't believe that Catriona would keep any money or securities in the house. Which left—what? Bills? Cancelled cheques? *Private papers?* Jaime's tongue clove to the roof of her mouth.

She went back to the desk and sat down. Until now, it had never occurred to her to look in the drawers of Catriona's desk for information. Until now, she would never have believed she was that kind of person, but the temptation to learn more about the woman who was her mother was too great. Besides, she thought bitterly, however much Catriona might try to deny it, she was her mother's daughter. And Catriona had never hesitated to do exactly as she liked.

As she had expected, a couple of the drawers in the desk were locked, but to her surprise the key didn't fit either one. Nor did she need it to open the lower cupboard. That door swung open to her touch to reveal nothing more incriminating than the computer-printed sheets of the manuscript.

Jaime frowned again, and looked about her. Now that she had started on this quest for the lock that the key fitted, she was loath to give up. The key had to open something. Why else would it have been on the floor? Unless Catriona had left it there deliberately, in the hope of catching her out.

Jaime gnawed at her lower lip. Apart from the desk, and the wood-framed filing cabinet, there was no other lock the key might fit. Catriona didn't lock her fridge or her drinks cupboard. And the key was much too small to fit a door.

She would have given up there and then, if her gaze hadn't been caught and held by the reflection of the pool rippling over one of Catriona's paintings. As she had noticed when she'd first arrived here, there were several paintings on the walls of the study. And she had seen enough movies to know that wall-safes were often hidden behind pictures. Was it possible? she wondered, looking down at the key again. Did she have the courage to find out?

A glance at her watch reassured her. It was after five—much too late for Sophie to think of bringing her afternoon tea. She guessed the taciturn housekeeper wouldn't bring her tea unless she asked for it. And Samuel was too much under her thumb to do so himself.

Taking a deep breath, she got to her feet again, and approached the nearest painting. It was a fairly simple matter to swing it away from the wall, although her heart palpitated a little as she did so. It had occurred to her that they might be individually alarmed.

They weren't, and a dozen paintings later Jaime had to admit defeat. If it was the key to a wall-safe, it wasn't hidden in the study. She frowned. As this house had originally belonged to Dominic's father, perhaps he'd realised how accessible the study was and had put it somewhere else.

The bedroom!

Jaime blinked as the thought occurred to her. Of course, no one with any sense would install a wall-safe in one of the ground-floor rooms. It was obvious it must be upstairs in Catriona's bedroom, the room she had shared with Lawrence Redding before he died.

Doubt assailed her. Apart from anything else, she wasn't absolutely sure where Catriona's suite of rooms was located. No one had ever shown her the layout of the house, and, although she had a vague idea of where the rooms were, to go looking on a trial and error basis would be foolish.

And yet...

Reassuring herself that apart from the servants she was alone in the house, Jaime came out of the study and, passing through her own small office, emerged into the corridor beyond. A wide expanse of Italian tile stretched towards the reception hall, where a curving balustraded staircase gave access to the upper floor.

Moistening her dry lips, Jaime quickly traversed the corridor and started up the stairs. She knew if she gave herself time to think about this she wouldn't go through with it. The idea that Catriona might be harbouring some secret information about her past was probably irrational anyway. Her mother had no reason to be sentimental about that period of her life.

A galleried landing almost encircled the hall below, but Jaime guessed that Catriona's rooms were situated at the end of one of the corridors that stretched away on either side. Double-panelled doors seemed to indicate the entrance to a suite, and, deciding she had nothing to lose, she chose the one on the right.

The corridor here was carpeted, probably to ensure that no footsteps could be heard in the rooms that opened from it. The walls, too, were lavishly covered with apricot silk, and there were more of the paintings Jaime had seen downstairs.

Despite herself, Jaime was nervous, and she had to fight down the urge to turn back. For heaven's sake, she chided herself, what did she have to lose? If Sophie should happen to come looking for her, she could always say she'd been curious to see where Catriona slept.

Nevertheless, the palms that reached for the round onyx doorknobs were damp with sweat, and she could feel her heart pounding in her chest. What if they thought she was a thief? What if they suspected she'd been stealing? Dear God, she had no wish to have to explain herself to anyone.

The doors opened into a cool, shaded sitting room. Probably to promote that coolness, the blinds had been left half-drawn, and the room was pale and shadowy in the afternoon light.

But at least it was empty, she saw at once, chiding

herself once again for her naivety. For heaven's sake, who had she expected to find here? A watching shade that might be her mother, or Lawrence Redding's ghost?

Taking a controlled breath, she turned and carefully closed the doors behind her. There was no point in inviting trouble, she assured herself firmly. Though what she intended to do wouldn't take very long.

There was little about the sitting room to indicate whose room it was. Sophie was very efficient at her job, and any abandoned article of clothing or discarded magazine had been neatly put away. The comfortable sofas, with their striped linen cushions and wooden arms, stood in silent splendour, facing polished cabinets, the contents of which could only be guessed at.

But, as Jaime had expected, there were pictures on these walls too, scenes of courtyards strewn with flowers, and lazy garden furniture, set against a backdrop of the ocean. And although she was fairly sure that what she was looking for wouldn't be here she saw no harm in checking before she invaded her mother's bedroom.

She had looked behind two of the paintings, and was in the process of lifting the third away from the wall, when a voice arrested her. 'What the hell do you think you're doing?' it snarled angrily, and the picture dropped from her nerveless fingers, to hang lopsidedly from its hook. It couldn't be Dominic, but it was, emerging grim-faced from what she guessed must be his bedroom, a towel wrapped about his middle, his hair soaked and trickling rivulets of water down his bare chest.

CHAPTER ELEVEN

THE anger Dominic felt at finding Jaime there was out of all proportion to the offence. He suspected that the reason he was here in Bermuda again was due in no small measure to the influence she had exerted on him, and to discover her in his sitting room, apparently checking out his paintings, made him feel slightly sick. Had he been wrong about her all along? Were her motives not as innocent as he'd thought?

She was stunned to see him; he could tell that from the look of horror on her face. But, dammit, what was Catriona doing while her secretary cased the joint? Where was she that Jaime had felt confident enough to invade his space?

'I—I—'

Her stammered attempt at an explanation didn't begin to mollify the rage he was feeling. When he'd arrived, he'd assumed Catriona and her secretary were working, and rather than get into lengthy explanations with his stepmother he had chosen to take a shower and freshen up before letting her know he was here. But now he wished he'd made his whereabouts known. It would certainly have avoided this situation.

'Well?' he growled, tightening the towel about his waist and advancing into the room. 'I asked you a civil question. Have the decency to give me an answer. I guess you thought I was safely out of the way.'

He saw her swallow. The spasmodic movement in her throat was a dead give-away, and he guessed it was to give her time to think. Though how she thought she could get out of this he couldn't imagine. As far as he could see, the facts were cut and dried.

'When—when did you get back?' she asked, instead of dealing with his question, and Dominic thought how typical it was of a woman to try and evade the point.

'An hour ago,' he snapped, determined not to let her divert his anger. 'Now, are you going to tell me what you were doing, or shall I call the police?'

'The police?'

She repeated his words in a high, squeaky voice, and although he despised himself for it an unwilling shred of sympathy stirred inside him. For the first time, he allowed himself to notice how deliciously feminine she looked in the sleeveless top and shorts, remembered her lush breasts, and long, long legs...

'Yes, the police,' he forced himself to say again, but without much conviction. 'Jaime, I've just caught you riffling this room like a common thief. Are you working on your own, or is there an accomplice lurking in the wings?'

Jaime's gasp seemed genuine. 'You can't think—' she began, and he gave her a retiring look.

'Can't think what?' he asked. 'That villains don't come in all shapes and sizes? That your innocent face precludes the fact that you could be guilty as hell?'

'I'm not!'

Her denial was energetic, but then it would be, he told himself irritably, steeling his heart. Dammit, there was no other explanation, and he was wasting his time pretending there was. 'Then what were you doing?' he demanded, with some reluctance. 'You thought I was away, so don't pretend you were looking for me.'

'I wouldn't. I wasn't.' She pressed her hands together at her waist, curling one balled fist into her palm. Then, as if it might appease him, she added, 'I thought—I thought these were—Catriona's apartments.'

'And that's an explanation?'

He was dripping water onto the carpet where he stood, which was the reason he gave himself later for why he chose to move towards her. His feet were wet, but as he stepped onto a patch of dry carpet her reaction to his involuntary movement caught him on the raw. She recoiled from him as if he'd hit her, as if his presence threatened her very existence. With a little gulp of what he readily recognised as panic, she stumbled back against the door. One fumbling hand sought blindly for the knob behind her and he knew if she got the door open she'd make her escape, and that would be that. There was no way he could tell Catriona what had happened, not without her turning it into something it was not.

He lunged forward, forgetting for a moment the precariousness of the towel wrapped about his waist. As his hand slammed against the panel beside Jaime's head, he felt the folds of cotton slip away. In consequence, when his body connected with hers, it wasn't there to protect him, and he was instantly aware of the soft fabric of her shorts against his skin.

It was absurdly sensual, but it wasn't the fine material that caused the blood to rush hotly to his loins. It was the feel of her limbs moving beneath the cloth that fired his emotions and made him breathless: the sensuous brush of her breasts against his chest.

For a moment, nothing was said. Dominic could hear her laboured breathing matching his own, and he strove hard to ignore the provocation of her struggling limbs. But her strength was being sapped by his weight, and she could obviously feel every stirring muscle in his body. And the more he tried to kill that thought, the more it disturbed him, so that very soon he was completely aroused.

But, God, it was so good to feel her warm body beneath him. For too many nights he'd imagined holding her this way, and the realisation was so much better than the dream. He knew he was in very real danger of losing complete control of his actions. He wanted her so badly, his hunger was becoming a physical pain.

'Please—'

Her soft breath fanned his throat, and her fists, balled against his midriff, made a futile attempt to push him away. His lips twisted. What did she think she could accomplish? he wondered bitterly. If she only knew how much he liked the feel of those slender hands against his skin. How tempted he was to edge them lower, closer to the source of the excitement that was driving him wild...

Jaime couldn't believe what was happening. She'd seen Dominic in the nude before—that morning when he'd risen out of the ocean like some pagan being—but she had never imagined she might one day be in this position. For God's sake, what was she to do? What could she say to make him release her? Particularly when, in spite of her fears, her heart was threatening to leap out of her chest.

'You didn't answer me,' he said, and she knew an insane desire to laugh. Surely he couldn't expect her to behave even marginally normally when his hairy thigh was wedged between her legs?

'I don't know what you want me to say,' she got out at last, trying hard not to meet his piercing gaze. 'You can't expect me to answer you in this situation. If you let me go, we might—'

'If I let you go, you'll be out of here so fast your feet won't touch the ground,' retorted Dominic hoarsely. 'Now, come on, what were you doing in here? Whether you thought this was Cat's room or not does not constitute a satisfactory explanation.'

Jaime's jaw worked. Despite the aggression in his tone, she was not unaware of the increasing pressure against her belly, and she realised that Dominic was far from being indifferent to her struggle, and that her actions were actually inflaming the situation. She sucked in a breath. He was aroused, and while the knowledge sent a wave of excitement surging through her veins the sane and sensible half of her brain was appalled that he should react in such a way.

'I—I wanted to see who had painted the picture!' she exclaimed, and at his sceptical look she insisted, 'I did. I—I'm interested in things like that.'

'So why didn't you ask Cat?' he demanded, and Jaime realised he had no idea that her mother wasn't here. Not that she had anything to gain by telling him that, she silently appended. If he guessed they were alone, he'd know he had nothing to fear.

'You—you'd better let go of me,' she said instead, her words in the nature of a warning, and she saw the flicker of recognition in his eyes.

'Oh?' he responded, but he made no move to do so. 'Why? What will you do if I don't? Tell Cat?' His lip curled. 'I'd like to be a fly on the wall when you tell her about this.'

'You need to get some clothes on,' she retorted, despising herself for not choosing to challenge him. 'Dominic, you're wetting me—'

'I am?' He drew back a space to look down at her, and she felt her nipples harden at that deliberately sensual appraisal. 'Oh, yes,' he murmured softly, 'I can see you might be uncomfortable.' He flexed his thigh, so that she couldn't help feeling the sensitive core of her womanhood riding against his damp leg. 'Well, I wouldn't want to spoil such a pretty outfit. Perhaps, like me, you ought to take your clothes off instead.'

'You're crazy!'

She was horrified at the reaction his words evoked— the heat that spread throughout her body and pooled with such intensity between her legs. She felt as if she was on fire, and as he continued to look at her the urge to rub herself against him was becoming overwhelming.

'I don't think so,' he said softly, and she guessed he was all too aware of her weakening emotions. 'It doesn't feel like that to me,' he commented pointedly. 'And perhaps I was wrong; perhaps you did come looking for me, after all. If so, you've got more—guts than I'd have given you credit for.'

Jaime's face flamed. She had never felt so mortified in her life, and the fact that he was a willing participant was little compensation. How could he say such things to her, she groaned silently, when he was Catriona's lover and this was Catriona's house? Had he no shame? Was he completely amoral? Or was he hoping she'd say something to incriminate herself, and thus justify his actions if he had to explain himself to her mother?

Her mother!

Catriona!

Jaime swallowed. She would have to tell him that Catriona was not here and risk the consequences. It was obvious that the older woman hadn't warned Dominic of what she intended to do before she'd left. Perhaps she'd suspected she might catch him out in some compromising situation, but even she could have had no expectation of this. Dear God, she would never believe that Jaime hadn't initiated her own seduction, and if Dominic was getting a little excited in the process, well, what the hell? he would argue disarmingly. He had never pretended to be a saint.

Even so, there was no denying she was attracted to him. No matter how she might deplore her feelings, she couldn't ignore them. The warmth of his skin, the strength that was keeping her so effortlessly where he wanted her, his arousal... She shivered. He was doing devastating things to her senses, and the scent of his maleness set the blood pounding in her head.

'You've got it wrong,' she blurted at last, realising she was on the brink of succumbing to the needs inside her. Any loyalty she might have felt towards Catriona was hard to sustain in the face of the pure carnality of his touch. She knew she was in an impossible situation, and doubted he would let her get away from him without her offering him something close to the truth. 'I didn't know you'd come back.'

'Yes. I can believe that.' His mouth was only inches away from hers now, moist, and gently mocking. 'What I want to know is why you felt so secure in invading my—or Cat's—privacy. Where is she, by the way? Did she take a convenient trip into town?'

'Something like that,' murmured Jaime unhappily, justifying the lie. But she knew with a feeling of shame that she wanted to feel that attractive mouth against hers again, and while she knew the chances she was taking the expectation seemed worth the risk.

'Mmm—very convenient,' conceded Dominic huskily, his own objectives being eroded by the physical needs of his body. Perhaps if he hadn't lost the towel he wouldn't have lost control so easily, but Jaime sensed her intrusion was no longer at the forefront of his mind.

She made one last attempt to hang onto her sanity, but when his tongue first lightly brushed her lips and then dipped between her teeth she was lost. The memory of the way he had kissed her on *Nightwing*, and the frantic lovemaking that had followed, was far too recent, and she abandoned herself to the heady possession of his mouth.

'Goddammit, I want you,' he said against her mouth, his lean-muscled frame pressing even closer. The damp heat of his skin penetrated the thin vest and shorts, and she could feel every curve and angle of his bones. One hand slid down her back to cradle the taut flesh of her rounded bottom, and her legs shook as he urged her more fully against him. If she'd been in any doubt as to his intentions, the hard strength of him thrusting against her stomach was proof enough.

'You can't,' she said, although she knew the words

were fatuous, and then gulped when she felt his other hand invade the waistband of her shorts.

'Why can't I?' he asked, with ruthless determination. 'It's what we both want. You know it. And no one need ever know.'

'No one' meaning Catriona, thought Jaime disgustedly, as abhorrent now of her behaviour as she'd already been of his. This meant nothing to him; it was just a means of assuaging his frustration. He wanted sex and she was available. Or at least that was what he thought.

'Let go of me,' she said fiercely, and although he obviously had no intention of doing so the tone of her voice did evoke some response.

'No way,' he said unsteadily, stroking her mouth with his thumb. 'I was a fool to let you go before. I won't make that mistake again.'

Disgust gave way to resignation. If Dominic was determined to have sex with her, there was little she could do to stop him. Besides, she tried to tell herself pragmatically, it wasn't as if she had never been with a man before. And, as her previous experiences had not led her to believe it was an experience she couldn't do without, what did she really have to lose?

Words like dignity and self-respect didn't mean much when she was in danger of betraying not only herself but also the woman who had once borne her. But something was warning her that if she let Dominic make love to her she might never find herself again.

'Dominic, please,' she begged. And then, less scrupulously, 'Your—my—Catriona may come back at any time!'

'Do you think I care?' he muttered hoarsely, his face buried in the scented hollow of her neck. 'And to think I thought you were such a nondescript creature the first time I saw you. How could I have been so wrong?'

Jaime trembled. 'I am,' she protested, her thighs quivering as his fingertips probed the cleft between her legs.

'I am—a nondescript creature,' she added, her breath catching in her throat. 'Oh, God, Dominic, don't do that! You have no right to treat me like a fool!'

The sound he made was half amused, half ironic. 'Is that what I'm doing?' he asked breathily, and she was again aware of something like self-deprecation in his tone. 'Oh, Jaime, don't sell yourself short. You're all woman. God help me, if anyone's a fool here, it's me.'

Jaime was at a loss for words. Despite all her misgivings, forebodings, whatever, her own feelings were way beyond control. No man had ever reduced her to such a state of hunger, and although she tried to detach her mind from what was happening to her body the dark tide of passion wouldn't ebb. She wanted him. It was a concept that was totally new to her, but she wanted him, and the wet heat that throbbed between her legs revealed her need.

His hands pushed the elastic waist of the shorts down so that it pressed hipster-like about the tops of her thighs. Why hadn't she worn any underwear? she berated herself, feeling the expanded band rubbing against the moist curls at the junction of her legs. Dear God, was she supposed to ignore what he was doing, or help him take her clothes off? With a supreme effort she suppressed the urge to press herself against him, though the hair wherein his manhood nested brushed provocatively against her own.

He was pushing her vest up now, exposing her puckered breasts to his avid gaze. 'Beautiful,' he muttered, bending to take one engorged nipple between his teeth. 'Now tell me you don't want me. Oh, Jaime—' he sucked powerfully at her breast '—your body gives you away every time.'

Jaime could hardly deny it, not when every nerve and sinew inside her was aching for a satisfaction it had never achieved. This is crazy, she told herself as he transferred his attention to her other breast, but it didn't make any difference. Her senses had taken over, and they weren't about to give up now.

Time stood still—or perhaps it raced, she couldn't be sure. All she was sure of was that her head was swimming, and her naked body felt silky soft against the coarser texture of his. It was a mindless awareness, summoning as it did an image of how they might look to an intruder watching them. But no one was likely to see them; Catriona was thousands of miles from here, and neither Sophie nor Samuel would save her if they could. Besides, she was no longer sure she wanted to be saved from an experience she'd waited for all her life.

Somehow—she never quite knew how—she found herself on the floor, with the cool weave of the carpet at her back. The indented wool dug into her buttocks, but it was not an unpleasant feeling. Besides, she was totally absorbed by the man kneeling between her thighs, spreading her legs apart and invading her wet core with a probing finger.

The sensation that caressing finger evoked knocked her dizzy for a moment, and although common sense might have favoured a different reaction she found herself arching up against him. She wasn't consciously aware of it, but she was endeavouring to repeat that dizzying sensation, wanting him to go on caressing her, to ease her already aching flesh.

'You see,' he said, with heavy-lidded eyes, seemingly enjoying the response he was getting. He bent again, and pressed his face to the vulnerable place his fingers had exposed, and she bucked against him wildly, convinced now she was beyond any hope of redemption.

'I—don't,' she said, when she could speak again, and the laugh he gave was soft and indulgent.

'Oh, I think you do,' he said, taking one of her hands and kissing the knuckles. Then he drew her hand to his body, folding her fingers around him. He gave a sudden intake of breath. 'So—so do I.'

He was so hot—that was her first realisation—and pulsing rapidly beneath her palm. Was it his heart she could feel? she wondered, taking the initiative and allowing the pad of her thumb to stroke the tip where a bead of moisture glistened. She looked at her thumb and knew a crazy desire to taste him, but before she could act upon it he jerked away.

'God!' His choked reaction to her caress fractured her thoughts, and almost desperately, it seemed, he captured her hand in his. 'Give me a break,' he muttered thickly, his voice hoarse and urgent, and then she felt his pulsing manhood against her.

For a moment it seemed an impossible task. In the heat of the moment, Jaime had never considered the mechanics of what he was about to do, and her muscles protested mightily at his invasion. 'God, are you a virgin?' he demanded, a moment before the powerful length of him filled her, but she refused to add to his conceit by denying it.

Still, in those first few moments she had to admit, to herself at least, that she had been apprehensive. So much so that when he started to move her nails dug into his arms, leaving tiny semicircles of redness in his flesh. Her throat felt tight, her breathing stifled, and for one awful moment she thought she was going to lose consciousness completely.

'Relax,' he chided her huskily, sensing her fears and neutralising them. He looked down to where their bodies were joined, an expression of pure indulgence on his face. 'We were made for each other,' he added softly, sliding a finger into her cleft, and, quickening his thrusts, he took them both beyond any chance—or desire—of drawing back...

CHAPTER TWELVE

DOMINIC came to his senses to find Jaime had wriggled out from under him, and was presently struggling to get into her clothes. Despite a momentary irritation that she should feel it necessary to underline the brevity of their encounter, the sight of those long, slim legs stepping into the clinging shorts was absurdly appealing. And sexy, he acknowledged drily, rolling onto his knees and reaching for one shapely ankle. 'What's the rush?' he demanded huskily, when she jerked almost fearfully beneath his hand. 'We've got the rest of the evening ahead of us. You said yourself that Cat doesn't know where you are.'

'That's not the point.' Somehow, perhaps because he was still feeling rather dazed at the strength of the feelings she had aroused in him, she managed to pull her ankle out of his grasp, and reached for her top. 'You should be ashamed of yourself,' she added, in a muffled voice, as the vest went over her head. 'My God, don't you care for—for Catriona at all?'

The accusation irritated him more than her aggravating attempt to run out on him had done, and he was tempted to show her how hollow her indignation was. She had been as hot to consummate their relationship as he had, no matter how she might regret her actions now.

And he found that that irritated him too. The fact that however unwilling she might have been in the beginning she couldn't deny that what had happened had been as much her fault as his. Well, almost, he conceded, with a latent sense of honesty. She shouldn't have been nosing around in his rooms, and when he had come on to her she shouldn't have melted like a snowflake beneath his hands.

'Of course I care for Catriona,' he bit out now, but like her protest earlier it had a hollow ring. The trouble was, when he was with Jaime, he had the devil's own job remembering what it was he had always seen in Catriona. He didn't want to admit it, but he was very much afraid infatuation had played the major part.

But that was crazy!

After all these years...

With a muffled snarl, he got to his feet, scowling as Jaime backed nervously away from him. For God's sake, what did she expect him to do to her now? Beat her because she'd given in? The temptation to avenge himself on someone was appealing, but he couldn't make her a scapegoat for his own sins.

'What are you going to do?'

Her husky voice could still ripple across his flesh like a drift of satin, and he bent to rescue the towel to avoid looking at her again. What *was* he going to do? he wondered grimly. When Catriona came back, how the hell was he going to face her after this?

The towel was lifted, and as it came up off the carpet something that glinted fell from its damp folds. He looked down, automatically covering the small metallic article with his foot when Jaime would have bent to rescue it. It was a key, he saw, when, after securing the towel about his waist again, he bent to pick it up. It wasn't his, so it must be Jaime's. She must have dropped it out of the pocket of her shorts.

With the key held firmly between his thumb and forefinger, he felt more confident to meet her gaze. 'Is this yours?'

'No—I mean, yes—' she fumbled, immediately arousing his suspicions. Goddammit, what did she have to be so nervous about? And why the hesitation in admitting it was hers?

'Either it is or it isn't,' he said, making no attempt to give it to her. He turned it from side to side. 'It's very small. What does it fit?'

Jaime took a breath. He saw her eyes dart around the room, and sensed the way she was evidently dying to snatch the key out of his grasp. And then a wave of comprehension hit him. It was the kind of key that might open a jewellery box. Catriona's jewellery box, perhaps. God, had she stolen it from her?

He blinked, trying to think. He remembered now that she'd said she'd thought this was Catriona's suite of rooms when he'd surprised her. Yet that still didn't explain why she'd been studying the pictures. Unless... He looked at the key again. Could she conceivably have thought it was a *safe* key? She didn't know Catriona very well if she thought his stepmother might keep anything of value in the house.

'I found it,' she said suddenly, breaking into his speculations. 'In—in the study downstairs. I—I was going to return it.'

'When?' asked Dominic tautly. 'When Cat comes home? Were you hoping to leave it in the lock?'

'I don't know what you mean.'

She held up her head, gazing at him with eyes that were clear and grey, and glistening with what he suspected might be unshed tears. Seeing them, he wanted to believe her, and he despised himself for being diverted from the truth.

'You thought it was a safe key,' he said, deciding he had nothing to lose in the present circumstances. She had only to tell Catriona what had happened and they'd both suffer the consequences. God, he must have been mad to risk everything for a moment's gratification. There was no way he was going to destroy his future—or the company's—for her.

'What do you mean?'

Her reply was not unexpected, and he could practically see her brain ticking over, trying to find a response. 'I mean I think you stole this from Cat,' he declared coldly. 'I can't imagine how you thought you'd get away with it.'

'Get away with a key?'

She was playing for time, but he humoured her anyway. 'Get away with stealing—*anything* from Cat,' he told her impatiently. 'Have you forgotten? Bermuda is an island. There's no place to hide.'

She gasped now. 'I'm not a thief!'

'Aren't you?' He tossed the small gold key on his palm. 'Then can you tell me what you were doing with this?'

'I've told you—'

'You were returning it? Yes? Well, I don't buy that, Jaime. And I have to tell you, if I relay that excuse to Cat, she won't believe it either.'

Jaime's face paled, and he knew a moment's compassion for the position she was in. The trouble was, it wasn't a simple position—for either of them—and he wished he didn't have his own guilt to contend with as well.

'I wasn't going to steal anything,' she insisted flatly. 'I don't care if you believe me or not. It's the truth.'

Dominic heaved a sigh. 'Jaime, you were looking for something in this room, and it wasn't the name of the artist who painted these pictures. Like you said, Cat's in town—'

Jaime raised up her head. 'She's not in town.'

'But you said she was.'

'No, you asked if she'd taken a—a convenient trip into town, and I said, Something like that.'

Dominic scowled. 'Stop playing with words. You knew what I meant. If she's not in town, where the hell is she?'

Jaime sniffed. 'New York.'

'New York!' Dominic stared at her. 'But I've just come from there.'

'I know that.' She shrugged. 'You must have passed in the air.'

He was stunned. 'Cat's gone to New York?' He shook his head. 'But why?'

'Why?' Now it was Jaime's turn to look disbelieving. 'Why do you think?'

Dominic swore.

'What's wrong?' For the moment she had the upper hand. 'Are you already anticipating her reaction when she realises you're not there? Or have I spoiled your evening's entertainment?'

'What the hell's that supposed to mean?'

He guessed she had spoken without thinking, and now her pale features suffused with colour. 'I'm sorry,' she said tautly. And then, with rather more spirit, she declared, 'It's nothing to do with me who you sleep with, is it?'

His jaw tightened. 'No, it's not,' he agreed tersely. And then, for no other reason than a need to justify himself, he added, 'And I don't sleep with Cat, if that's what you're implying.'

Patently, she didn't believe him, and he knew a perverse desire to pretend she was right. Not for the first time, he realised how unlikely his relationship with Catriona was, and he had to ask himself why he had waited so long...

'That doesn't mean I haven't wanted to,' he said now, almost as a defence. 'She's a woman any man would be proud to possess, but my father's only been dead a year.'

Jaime's lip curled. 'You don't have to explain yourself to me,' she said, and he realised how neatly their positions had been reversed.

'No, I don't,' he snapped, angered that he should have forgotten how this had started. 'You, on the other hand, have still to convince me you're not a crook.'

Jaime's expression altered, and she sighed. 'How am I supposed to do that?' she protested, clearly wishing he would move away from the door. 'I've told you the truth. I found the key in the study. I was working on the files when I saw it on the floor behind the cabinet.'

'That still doesn't explain what you were doing up here.' Dominic was growing tired of this verbal lunge and parry. 'Why don't you admit that you were prying, at the very least? As Cat's not here, you had no right to enter these apartments, whether you thought they were hers or not.'

Jaime expelled a weary sigh. 'All right.'

'All right—what?'

'All right, I was prying,' she declared steadily. 'What are you going to do about it?'

Dominic's scowl deepened. 'I don't know.'

'Oh, great!'

'I have to think about this,' he retorted sharply. 'I have to ask myself what you might have done if you'd found whatever this key opens. I take back what I said earlier. You could have stolen something valuable, and been off the island before Cat got back.'

'Oh, please—'

'It's true. Only I turned up and—and—'

'And what?' she broke in harshly now. 'And caught me red-handed? And arrested me? And *seduced* me?'

'I didn't seduce you.' He resented the connotation.

'What would you call it, then?' she demanded indignantly. 'I wasn't exactly willing when you forced yourself on me.'

'I didn't force myself on you,' he snarled. 'And you weren't exactly *un*willing either. Perhaps I was just finishing what we started. I got the feeling you were pretty disappointed with my behaviour on the yacht.'

Now why had he said that? Why had he reminded her of something he had tried to forget? Out of the mouths of fools, he thought, cursing his careless tongue. She was staring at him as if he'd just crawled out from under the nearest stone, and he doubted anything he said now could put things right.

'You bastard,' she said at last, scrubbing the knuckles of one hand across her cheek as she did so. 'You bastard!' She sniffed resentfully. 'I've a good mind to tell Catriona—everything.'

'Go ahead.'

Dominic's eyes narrowed, and he marvelled at his ability to court disaster so assiduously. Was it only moments ago that he'd wanted to finish this? Right now, there seemed no avenue for escape.

Jaime held up her head. 'You don't think she'd believe me, do you?' she persisted, and he admired the way she'd recovered her composure. Reluctantly, too, he was aware of his own rekindled attraction for her, and of how crazy it was to pursue this when it was Catriona that he wanted.

'Does it matter what I think?' he asked, ignoring the provocation in her voice. He took a deep breath. 'I guess this isn't the time or the place to discuss it. I suggest we give ourselves some breathing space.'

'You won't change my mind.'

There was an edge of hysteria to her voice now and Dominic suppressed the urge to tell her she had his blessing. For God's sake, what did she think she'd achieve by threatening him? In his present mood, there was nothing she could say that could make him feel any worse.

Taking the line of least resistance, he made no response to her outburst, starting instead for the bathroom. He seemed to remember he'd left a shirt and shorts hanging on the back of the door, and he needed the protection they could give.

'Don't you care?'

Her cry held all the elements of frustration, and Dominic wondered what she wanted him to say. 'If it's what you want to do, I can't stop you,' he declared flatly. 'But you do realise it will mean you'll lose your job?'

Jaime's horrified gasp reached him as his hand closed on the handle of the bathroom door. 'You're completely without conscience, aren't you? Is this what happened to Kristin? Did you seduce her, too?'

'I never laid a hand on Kristin,' Dominic snapped, anger reasserting itself again. 'And I'd be careful how you throw your accusations about, if I were you. You've got no proof I ever touched you. And Catriona's not known for her generosity where other women are concerned.'

'As you would know.'

'I warn you, Jaime——'

'Yes?' She took a defiant step towards him, and he had the curious notion that she wanted him to lose his temper with her. 'Are you threatening me, Mr Redding?' she goaded. 'Did I finally strike a nerve? Well, you may think you're very clever, but perhaps I know something even you don't know.'

'What?'

Doubt clouded her eyes now. 'What?' she echoed, almost as if she regretted having challenged him. 'I don't know what you mean.'

'You said there was something even I didn't know,' he reminded her curtly. 'Stop playing games, Jaime. We both know you're just trying to distract me from the real reason you were trespassing in these rooms.'

She rallied. 'Do we?'

'Yes.'

Her lips twisted. 'Well——' She shrugged, and seemed to change her mind again. 'You're probably right.'

Her sudden acquiescence was as implausible as her defiance had been earlier. 'So you admit you've been lying all along?' he taunted, hoping to rekindle her indignation. What had she been implying? he wondered. Had Catriona told her something he should know?

'You don't know anything,' she snapped. 'But maybe you're right. Maybe I was looking for something. The proof that blood is thicker than water, even here.'

Dominic was baffled. 'What's that supposed to mean?' he asked impatiently. 'Cat and I aren't related. You know that.'

'I never said you were.' Once again, Jaime looked as if her tongue had run away with her. 'Look, can I go now? I've got a whole host of files to put away—'

'Not until you explain what you meant about blood being thicker than water, *even here*,' he declared flatly. 'You're not telling me you're Cat's long-lost sister, are you?' His lips curved. 'Oh, God, that would make things a little difficult, wouldn't it?'

His sarcasm infuriated her; he could see it, and something about her expression gave him pause. 'God, she is your sister, isn't she?' he exclaimed incredulously. 'No wonder I thought you reminded me of her.'

'She's not my sister!'

Jaime's gasp of outrage silenced him, and he stared at her with disbelieving eyes. 'Then what—?'

'She's my mother!' cried Jaime fiercely, and then uttered a desperate groan. 'At least—at least, I thought she might be,' she mumbled unhappily, and he could tell from her expression that she was already regretting having admitted as much to him.

CHAPTER THIRTEEN

OH, GOD, why had she said that?

Jaime paced restlessly about the sitting room of her apartments, trying to come to terms with what had happened. Apart from anything else, she had destroyed any chance of a relationship between her and her mother—though perhaps that was irrelevant after what she'd done.

Everything that had happened since she'd found the key and left Catriona's study had assumed the qualities of a nightmare. She couldn't believe that Dominic had made love to her; she couldn't believe that she'd betrayed her mother's secret in that way.

She knew it had been the cavalier manner in which he had dismissed what had happened that had hurt her. For the first time in her life, she'd known a quite unholy desire to have her revenge. But telling him that Catriona was her mother had been quite unforgivable. It wasn't her mother's fault that she'd been such a fool.

She sighed. Why hadn't she let him go on thinking she was not to be trusted? That way, she would have had an excuse for leaving before her mother got back. As it was, she could only hope to practise damage limitation. She doubted she would have felt any more raw and abused if he had called the police.

And as soon as the words had left her mouth she'd known they would achieve nothing. She'd let him rile her, and now she was paying the price for answering back. Somehow she would have to stop him telling Catriona. Whatever happened in the future she knew her mother would never forgive her if she found out.

If only, she thought futilely. If only she'd never found

the key; if only she'd never thought of searching Catriona's rooms; if only Dominic had still been in New York...

She thought the road to hell must be paved with 'if onlys'. Like good intentions, they never did achieve a positive end. And when all was said and done she had been discovered in a compromising situation. If Dominic had taken advantage of that, she had only herself to blame.

He had been right, after all: she hadn't put up much of a fight. She might resent his insinuations, but there was no doubt that she hadn't discouraged him from making love to her. In all honesty, she'd wanted him in a way she had never imagined she could want any man.

But that was no excuse for betraying her mother; betraying herself, too, if it came to that. She'd acted like a schoolgirl, not a woman. She shook her head. Since she'd arrived in Bermuda, she had hardly been able to recognise herself anymore.

She paused at the window, gazing out over the balcony to the darkening line of the ocean, glistening in the fading light. It was almost dark, and—she glanced at the watch on her wrist—in fifteen minutes Dominic was expecting her to join him for supper. For supper, she thought wildly, the tide of panic rising inside her again. How could they sit down to supper together as if nothing had happened?

Yet when she'd left his room she'd been grateful for the respite, however brief. Even though he had insisted that they continue the discussion later and, consequently, it had been agreed that they should have supper together, an arrangement with which Jaime had been virtually forced to comply.

She glanced at her watch again, and saw that the minute hand was fast approaching Dominic's deadline. He would expect an explanation, and she had to give it to him. But what she was going to say was another matter.

She had no right to tell him anything. It wouldn't make her situation any better, and she could only hope to bluff her way out of the mess she had created.

She was late for the meal. Their places had been set at right angles at the end of the long table in the dining salon, and when Jaime arrived, flushed and apologetic, her hair still damp from the shower she had hurriedly taken, Dominic was already seated in his place.

He rose to his feet at her entrance, however, politely acknowledging her arrival by his actions if not by the sombre expression upon his face. Like her, he had evidently spent the time considering what she'd told him, but she couldn't tell from his appearance what his conclusions had been.

'I'm sorry,' she said as she sat down, and Samuel, who had been hovering by the door, slipped away to warn Sophie they were ready to eat. She licked her lips. 'I'm afraid I forgot the time,' she added, needing to distract herself from her awareness of his leanly muscled body. In a dark green silk shirt and black chinos, he looked every bit as attractive as before.

'I doubt that.' His response was sardonic, and without looking at her he lifted the bottle of wine beside his plate and poured a measure of the rich liquid into her glass. She noticed he refilled his own glass with rather more liberality. Perhaps he thought he needed it more than she did. Of that, Jaime had her doubts.

'It's true,' she said, raising her glass and looking at him over the rim. She inhaled. 'Mmm, this is nice. What is it?'

'Château Rothschild '82 or '83; does it matter?' he snapped ill-humouredly. He swallowed another mouthful of his own wine, and then regarded her with narrow-eyed intent. 'Perhaps I thought a special vintage was warranted. It's not every day you learn that your fiancée has a grown-up daughter.'

Jaime caught her breath, but before she could think of

a response Sophie arrived with their first course. Jaime prayed the housekeeper hadn't heard Dominic's careless pronouncement, and she was relieved to see that Sophie seemed more intent on the way the food was presented than anything else.

The salad of pear and goat's cheese with a cranberry vinaigrette was delicious, a sprinkling of toasted walnuts adding a crunchy texture to the sauce. There was oatmeal bread, too, richly coated with sesame seeds, and some of the yellow island butter served fresh from the churn.

For all her anxiety, Jaime ate hungrily, the roast lamb and parsley potatoes that followed acting as a kind of palliative to her nerves. By the time she had swallowed a generous helping of sherry trifle she was feeling decidedly less empty, and she understood what people meant about eating to compensate.

Conversely, she noticed that Dominic ate little and drank a lot. It was obvious he was impatient for the meal to be over so that he could get some answers to the questions he was eager to ask. He even eschewed having any coffee, opening another bottle of wine instead.

Jaime accepted Samuel's offer of coffee, however. Anything to postpone the confrontation that was to come. With the coffee served, there was no further reason for either Sophie or Samuel to linger, though Jaime intercepted the approving look that passed between Dominic and the housekeeper as she departed.

'So,' he said, when the candles that supplemented the lamps had been lit, and the housekeeper and her husband had withdrawn to their quarters, 'perhaps you'd like to explain. How can Cat be your mother? She must have been little more than a schoolgirl when you were born.'

Not quite, thought Jaime ruefully, but she kept that particular comment to herself. 'I—I never actually said she was—my mother. I said—I'd thought—she might be. That was all.'

'That isn't quite how I remember it,' he retorted

crisply, 'but we'll let that go for now. What I want to know is why you even suspected the relationship. Have you discussed this with anyone else?'

'No.'

'No?' Dominic's brows arched interrogatively. 'Not even with Cat herself?'

'No.'

'Why not?'

Jaime caught her upper lip between her teeth. 'I told you—I wasn't sure—'

His eyes were sharp. 'Well, I find that incredible. Asking the other person involved is the most natural course there is.'

'In normal circumstances, perhaps.' Jaime swallowed uncomfortably. 'As I say, I wasn't sure. Can't we leave it at that?'

'No, we bloody can't.' Dominic scowled, and she noticed the tell-tale tinges of red around his eyes. Obviously, the wine he'd drunk at supper was not the only alcohol he'd consumed since her bald announcement. 'You shouldn't have mentioned it at all if that's the case.'

'I know that.'

'Well?'

'You—you goaded me into it.'

'I goaded you!'

'Yes.' She took a breath. 'Threatening me with losing my job if I exposed you to Catriona. You just think you can use people—women—and they won't answer back.'

Dominic scowled. 'I didn't *use* you.'

'No?' Now it was her turn to look sceptical.

His mouth compressed. 'What happened—well, it wasn't meant to happen, if that's any consolation.' He paused. 'Whatever you think, I'm not in the habit of—of—'

'Seducing women?'

'Of cheating on the woman I love.'

Jaime quivered. 'If you say so.'

'I do say so.' He swallowed another mouthful of his wine. 'But we're getting away from the point.'

'I thought that was the point.' Jaime tried to be flip, but it didn't quite come off.

'No. The point is, why should you think Catriona was your mother? You came here—presumably under an assumed name—to take this job as her assistant. Wasn't that a fairly reckless thing to do if you had no proof?'

Jaime sighed. 'Perhaps I felt like a change of scene.'

'Perhaps you did.' He regarded her steadily. 'Perhaps you were so angry with me, you made the whole thing up. So why do I get the feeling you're still lying? Jaime, for pity's sake, can't you tell me the truth?'

'I am telling you the truth.' Jaime hesitated. 'Like I said, you made me angry.'

'So angry that you devised this whole story just to get your own back?'

'I didn't say that.'

'Then what are you saying?' He gazed at her frustratedly. 'What did I do except prove that you wanted me every bit as much as I wanted you?'

'Is that your excuse?' Jaime eyed him tremulously. 'And I've said all I'm going to say on the subject. I wish I'd never found that blasted key.'

'So do I,' muttered Dominic sourly, around another mouthful of his wine. 'You might be interested to know that the key did fit Catriona's jewel box. But that doesn't alter the fact that I wish I'd never left New York.'

Jaime's lips twisted. 'Because you'd have been with—with Catriona now instead of me?'

'Because life wouldn't have been so complicated,' he retorted, looking suddenly weary. He probably considered what had happened the biggest mistake of his life.

'Anyway, it doesn't matter about that,' he continued impatiently. 'You expect me to ignore everything you've said about Cat, is that right?'

'It would be easier,' Jaime murmured, praying he meant it. 'Um—are you sure you don't want any coffee? There's heaps still in the pot—'

'To hell with the coffee.' He stared at her broodingly. 'What about the likeness between you?'

She faltered. 'Well—I suppose I did wonder,' she offered lamely. 'My—my own mother abandoned my— me—abandoned me when I was just a baby, and I've always wondered what happened to her. When—when I saw Miss Redding's picture on the jacket of one of her books, I suppose I wanted her to be the person I thought she was.'

Dominic scowled. 'You expect me to believe that on the strength of a photograph you threw up a perfectly good job and came here to find out?'

'Perhaps.'

'And when I caught you in what you thought was Cat's room you were just playing detective, trying to find some clue to prove she was who you thought she was?'

Jaime hesitated. 'Maybe.'

'So why didn't you say so? What were you afraid of? That I might object to Cat's having an illegitimate daughter?' He didn't notice her sudden intake of breath as he continued, 'Oh, Jaime, you don't know me very well. If—when—Cat and I get it together, I won't care what she did before she married my father.'

Jaime couldn't speak. It had never occurred to her that he might think her parents hadn't been married, but perhaps it was all for the best. He could hardly ask Catriona if she'd got a divorce if he didn't know about her first husband.

'So—what are you thinking now?' He was staring at her again, and Jaime struggled to adopt a neutral expression. 'You're not still harbouring the notion that it might be true?'

'I—no—'

'If it's any consolation, Cat has always regretted the

fact that she and my father never had any children.' His eyes narrowed. 'She always insisted she was to blame, him having had me, you see.'

'I see.'

Jaime didn't want to hear any more of this. It was more than enough to know that her mother had denied her existence all these years. She didn't want to hear the lies Catriona had told Dominic about her relationship with his father.

She took a mouthful of her wine, feeling the rich liquid sliding comfortingly down into her stomach. Tendrils of heat spread into her legs, and she tried not to think about what she had learned. It wasn't his fault—or his father's—that Catriona had deceived them. And what were a few years deducted from her age compared to all the rest she had to hide?

The candlelight flickered, creating an intimate ambience in the room. If Dominic hadn't been watching her so closely, she might have drawn some comfort from the sympathy she sensed was lurking in his eyes.

He had such beautiful eyes, she thought treacherously. Given all that had gone before, she ought not to have found anything about this man to please her gaze. But she did; and the knowledge that after tonight they were unlikely to spend any time alone together was devastating.

'Well?' he probed, when she remained silent, and she realised he was waiting for her to say something more.

'As you say,' she mumbled at last, 'it was a foolish idea. In fact...' she paused to take another sip of her wine '...I think the more sensible course is for me to leave immediately. The probationary two weeks is almost over, and I've decided I'm not cut out for this kind of work, after all.'

Dominic's nostrils flared. 'You can't.'

Jaime trembled. 'What do you mean—I can't? When

Miss Redding employed me, it was on the understanding that at the end of two weeks—'

'I mean—' Dominic's fist balled beside his plate. 'I mean you can't leave until Cat gets back.' He met her startled gaze. 'It's the least you can do, in the circumstances. She might want you to stay until she can find a replacement.'

No way, thought Jaime painfully, but she kept that thought to herself. There was no way she was going to remain here any longer than her contract demanded. She wished she didn't have to see Catriona and Dominic together ever again.

CHAPTER FOURTEEN

DOMINIC awakened with a hangover, and the uneasy conviction that events were moving out of his grasp. What had happened to the clear-eyed vision he had always had of his future? Suddenly everything he'd believed about himself was being put to the test.

He knew Jaime Harris's arrival—was that her real name?—had something to do with it. Quite a lot to do with it, in fact, he acknowledged grimly, drawing one leg up to rest the sole of his foot against the fine linen sheet. Until she'd entered his life, he hadn't felt the need to defend himself to anyone. And his relationship with Catriona—sterile though it was—had been the only thing that mattered to him.

All that had changed.

And not for the better, he brooded irritably. Slowly, but surely, Jaime was undermining every decision he tried to take. If he was honest he'd admit that she was the reason he'd returned to Bermuda, not Catriona. He'd sensed that her association with his stepmother might not survive much longer, and he'd wanted to see her again before she left.

And why? he asked himself scornfully. The scowl that never seemed far from his lean features these days returned to stab a crease between his eyes. So that he could finish what he'd started on *Nightwing*. So he could satisfy himself that she couldn't possibly be as sensual as he remembered.

His scowl deepened. If he'd been that desperate for a woman, why hadn't he wanted Catriona? The Lord knew she'd been begging him to make love to her for months.

Months when he'd always found an excuse not to give
in to her demands; when he'd rather have paid for the
privilege with a stranger than seek solace in her bed.

The infuriating thing was, he should never have
touched Jaime—wouldn't have touched her, he assured
himself, if she hadn't come to his room and found him
naked as the day he was born. He might have wanted to
see her again, he admitted unwillingly, but he wasn't
stupid. He cared for Catriona; he respected her; and playing around with her assistant was just asking for trouble.

Yet...

He stubbed his toe against the mattress, loath to accept
that even the knowledge that Catriona might walk in on
them hadn't stopped him from slaking his lust in Jaime's
firm young body. Far from carrying her to his bed, he'd
treated her like some cheap hooker, taking her on the
floor like a stag in rut.

And what about that story she'd devised about
Catriona maybe being her mother? Had it really only
been an excuse to explain why she was searching his
bedroom, or did she believe it might conceivably be
true? Whatever, it made no difference to his own situation. He'd jeopardised all he'd always hold dear for a
few minutes' sexual gratification with a woman who despised him.

The realisation that the sun was higher than he'd
imagined, seeping through the top slats of his blind with
a strength it didn't usually possess until later in the
morning, had him turning his head to look at the clock
on his bedside cabinet. Dammit, he swore impatiently,
it was nearly eleven o'clock. His body clock must have
been addled by the amount of alcohol he had consumed
after Jaime had gone to her rooms. And it had been after
midnight before he'd tumbled into bed.

Even so, it was with some reluctance that he pushed
himself up from his pillows. The temptation to remain
where he was, to delay facing his problems until later in

the day, was strong, but he had no doubt Catriona would be coming back from New York this morning. She'd probably booked her flight as soon as she'd found he wasn't there. The miracle was she hadn't chartered a plane and flown back the night before. Cat was nothing if not single-minded when it came to getting her own way.

After peering through the blind and finding the pool area deserted, Dominic stumbled into his bathroom and took a cold shower. The water was never icily cold, as it was in New York, but it was refreshing, and after towelling himself dry and pulling on a black cotton T-shirt and bleached denim cut-offs he left his room.

It didn't surprise him that Sophie hadn't awakened him. Too many occasions when she'd been bawled out for her trouble had taught the housekeeper to keep a low profile when he'd been drinking. He wasn't proud of himself, but these past few months had been a drain on his nerves. Maintaining his distance with Catriona wasn't as easy as it might look.

The query as to why he should want to keep his distance with Catriona raised its head again, but Dominic firmly tamped it down. Now definitely wasn't the time to be having doubts of that sort, and he ignored the small voice that warned him he would have to face it soon.

Samuel was in the hall, assiduously sweeping the marble tiles, his brush moving in slow, mesmerising strokes. For a moment, Dominic envied him his uncomplicated existence, but then common sense told him it was shame he was feeling, not envy.

'Morning, sir.'

Samuel stopped what he was doing to offer the greeting, always deferential when Sophie wasn't around. The housekeeper, conversely, considered herself a member of the family, and with the familiarity of long years' service was more likely to say exactly what she thought.

'Good morning,' Dominic answered, glancing briefly

into the sitting room. 'Um—do you know where Miss
Harris is? Is she working in Miss Redding's study?'

Samuel clasped both hands around the end of the handle, and rested his chin on his knuckles. His delay in
answering should have warned Dominic that he was reluctant to do so, but his words still came as something
of a shock.

'She's gone, sir,' he said uncomfortably, shrugging his
bony shoulders. 'She left straight after breakfast. Didn't
you know?'

Dominic stifled the cutting retort that sprang to his
lips at the old man's words. It was obvious Samuel knew
he hadn't been aware of the fact, and he hated being
humoured. But the knowledge that Jaime had just
walked out, not just on him but on Catriona too, infuriated him. Humiliated him too, although he didn't want
to examine that.

'No, I didn't know,' he said now, with studied polite-
ness. 'Where did she say she was going? Do you know?'

'Back to England, I assume. I can't say I'm particularly interested,' drawled a third, all too familiar voice.
'Good morning, darling. You must have been tired. I've
said it before: you work far too hard these days.'

The flight from Atlanta landed at Gatwick just after
seven a.m. Jaime, who had been *en route* for the best
part of twenty-four hours, was exhausted when she
stepped off the plane. Despite the time of year, it had
been a rather bumpy Atlantic crossing, and that, added
to her general feeling of unease, had made it impossible
for her to sleep.

The airport was cool at that time of the morning, dou-
bly so to someone coming back from a semi-tropical
heat. Jaime shivered as she hoisted her carry-on bag and
made her way to where the carousels would deliver her
suitcase. But it was an inner chill she was feeling that
had nothing to do with the temperature of the air.

Outside, the morning promised to be more inviting. It was still cold, of course, but the sky was clearing, and Jaime thought it might be a fine day. She would have to get the windows opened and the house aired, she thought, trying to be practical. And go to the supermarket. There might be a couple of instant meals in the freezer, but she'd need some bread and other staple foods.

The taxi driver who transported her into town was friendly. 'You look brown,' he said. 'Been somewhere nice?'

'Bermuda,' answered Jaime pleasantly, determining not to let what had happened make her bitter. 'Have you ever been there?'

'No such luck,' answered the driver, grimacing. Then he frowned. 'But didn't you just get off the Atlanta flight?'

'I—yes. I made a detour.' Jaime felt herself colouring. She could hardly tell him she'd boarded the first plane that had had a vacant seat.

Fortunately, he didn't ask why she'd detoured to Atlanta, and it was easy enough to guide the conversation onto other things. She had been away for two weeks, after all, and she was interested in what had been happening in her absence, even if a terrorist bomb was the topic on everyone's lips.

The house in Allison Road was stuffy. Several days of warm weather had robbed the rooms of any fresh air, and a particularly unpleasant smell in the kitchen revealed an opened carton of milk she'd omitted to throw away.

Emptying the offending substance into the downstairs toilet, Jaime felt a wave of nausea sweep over her. But it wasn't just the smell of the sour milk; her stomach had been churning long before she'd entered the house.

She was probably hungry, she decided, and, returning to the kitchen, spooned coffee into the filter, and left it to heat while she went upstairs. The windows there needed opening too, and she felt a certain amount of relief in unpacking in her own bedroom again. She was home, she told herself firmly. She'd done what she'd set out to do, and now she could get on with the rest of her life. She'd soon forget Catriona—and Dominic. They had no part in her future, and the sooner she put what had happened behind her, the easier it would be.

She found an unopened packet of biscuits in the cupboard and several of them, with a cup of black coffee, drove the worst pangs of nausea away. She should have eaten the breakfast they'd offered on the plane, she acknowledged ruefully, but despite the time here her body clock was telling her it was still barely six a.m. in Bermuda.

In Bermuda...

Her lips trembled, and she determinedly pressed them together. She'd get over it, she assured herself firmly. It wasn't as if she'd cared for Dominic at all. And she'd known Catriona wasn't satisfied with her before she'd left for New York. Finding the files Jaime had been working with spread all over her desk had provided Catriona with the perfect excuse to get her out of the house.

And, dammit, she had already decided to leave, Jaime reminded herself painfully. After what had happened between her and Dominic, there was no way she could have stayed on. She'd behaved like a fool, and now she was going to have to pay for it. And at least she wasn't going to be a whipping boy, for either of them.

But finding her mother waiting for her at the breakfast table the previous morning had been quite a shock. As when Dominic had appeared the day before, she'd had no warning of Catriona's arrival, and finding her mother sitting there when she'd been half prepared to see Dominic had brought the hot colour pouring into her cheeks.

'There's no need to look so embarrassed, Miss Harris.' Catriona's tone had possessed all the warmth of an Arctic winter. 'I realise you didn't expect me back so soon, but I hardly anticipated that you'd invade my room in my absence.'

Jaime's lips parted. 'Your room?' she echoed faintly. *But it had been Dominic's room; he'd said so.*

'Yes, my room,' repeated Catriona sharply. 'Don't stand there looking so dumb. The files, Miss Harris: they're all over my desk. How am I supposed to work when I'm surrounded by your obvious inefficiency?'

'Oh, the files!' Belatedly Jaime was aware that there had been far too much relief in her voice.

'What else?' demanded Catriona, her blue eyes fixed and glacial. 'Don't tell me you've damaged the word processor. That's an expensive piece of equipment, and—'

'I haven't—damaged anything,' muttered Jaime uneasily, aware that Catriona's gaze was disturbingly intent. 'And as you'd asked me to work on the files I thought you'd have no objection to me using your desk. After all, the files are all in your study.'

'Where they belong,' declared Catriona curtly. 'But you could have moved them into your room while I was away. Instead of which, you've made my room look like a warehouse. It won't do, Miss Harris. It simply won't do.'

'No.'

Jaime acknowledged the reproof calmly, wondering if this was the way Catriona usually dealt with her employees. In other circumstances, she might have been tempted to defend herself more enthusiastically, but as things were it was probably easier to let Catriona throw her out.

'Is that all you have to say for yourself?' Catriona had clearly expected a different response. 'Don't you think a few words of apology might be in order? After all, I trusted you, Miss Harris. I don't like to think of you riffling through my private papers in my absence.'

'I wasn't riffling through your private papers!' denied Jaime hotly, though the accusation had been unpleasantly close to the truth. 'I—I was doing what you pay me for. If—if anyone's said anything else…'

Catriona's narrow brows arched. 'Who else is there?' Her lips curled. 'Sophie? I think not.'

'Not Sophie,' Jaime protested, wondering if Catriona was being deliberately obtuse. 'I—I meant—Dominic.' She coloured at the blatantly casual use of his name. 'I—suppose that's why you cut your trip short.'

'Dominic?'

The silence that followed should have warned Jaime she had made a tactical mistake. 'Mr Redding,' she said, completely misinterpreting Catriona's reaction. 'He was really—disappointed when he found you weren't here.'

'Really?' Catriona's lips were thin and drawn. 'And when did—Dominic arrive?'

'Um—yesterday afternoon—I think.' Jaime's throat felt unpleasantly dry. 'I assumed—I mean, I naturally thought you knew.'

'Obviously not.' Catriona's words were civil enough, but Jaime sensed she was furious inside. Then, as if adjusting her words to the situation, she added tightly, 'I suppose—as he wasn't at his office—I should have guessed.'

Jaime licked her lips. 'You—you didn't tell him you were going to New York, then?'

Catriona stiffened. 'I—I wanted to surprise him,' she declared tersely. She forced a cold smile. 'It seems I did.'

'Yes.'

Jaime didn't know what else to say, and presently Catriona returned to the attack again. 'It didn't occur to you to try and ring me? You have the number of my

apartment. Wouldn't that have been the most sensible
thing to do?'

Probably, thought Jaime ruefully, but the circumstances in which she had discovered Dominic's whereabouts had left little room for sensible reasoning.

'I never thought,' she admitted, deciding she had
nothing to lose. 'Um—when did you get back? This
morning?'

'Late last night, as it happens.' Catriona regarded her
without liking. 'Not that it's any concern of yours. I
think you must agree, Miss Harris, we are not going to
suit one another, after all. I suggest you make arrangements to return to England. Naturally, I'll pay your ex-
penses back to London.'

Jaime exhaled a trembling breath. So this was it! Now
that it had actually happened, she found she wasn't as
resolved about leaving as she'd thought. She'd come
here to get to know the woman she believed to be her
mother, and now she was contemplating leaving without
telling her who she was.

'You'll have some breakfast, of course.'

Now that she had got her own way, Catriona could
afford to be magnanimous, and although the last thing
Jaime wanted at this moment was food she found herself
grasping the back of the chair opposite and sitting down.
'Thank you,' she said, accepting the other woman's offer
of coffee, but then the breath caught in her throat when
she noticed the ring Catriona was wearing on her middle
finger.

It wasn't an expensive ring, but it was pretty: a small
cluster of diamonds surrounding an equally small sapphire. And the design was familiar, too familiar to miss.
She'd seen that ring very recently, on the photograph
her father had kept.

She breathed deeply. Maybe at any other time she
wouldn't have recognised it. It wasn't as if the design
was original, and on anyone else she wouldn't have

given it a second glance. But it was only a short while since she'd examined that old wedding photograph, and despite its attractiveness it was such an unlikely bauble for Catriona to wear.

She went for much more costly jewellery—solitaires, and rubies and emeralds set in diamond clusters. There was no reason for her to own such an inexpensive item, except that it had been her engagement ring, the ring Robert Michaels had given her.

Jaime stifled the sob that rose in her throat at the realisation. Catriona's jewel case might have been able to answer her questions, after all. That key she'd found might have proved crucial, if Dominic hadn't appeared and driven all other thoughts out of her head.

'Is something wrong?'

Catriona had noticed her distress, and was regarding her closely, and Jaime realised she was in danger of giving herself away. But, dammit, she thought, she should not leave without saying anything. Particularly not now she'd recognised the ring.

'Um—there's something I want to say,' she began awkwardly, feeling the hot colour rising up her neck, but before she could go on Catriona interrupted her.

'I hope this isn't going to be what I think it is,' she declared, her eyes narrowed and suspicious. 'I've said I'll make sure you don't lose by the situation, but if you attempt to threaten me—'

'To threaten you?' Jaime was appalled. 'I don't know what you mean.'

'Oh, I think you do.' Catriona sniffed. 'Kristin threatened me with a similar personal exposé. Well, I warn you, I won't be intimidated. As I told Kristin when she left, if you want to tell the world about my relationship with Dominic, then go ahead.'

Jaime's jaw sagged. 'I never thought of such a thing.' Besides, if what Dominic had said was true—and she found she badly wanted to believe him—he and Catriona didn't have a relationship. *Yet.*

'In any case,' continued her mother complacently, just as if Jaime hadn't spoken, 'everyone's going to hear about it very soon. He's asked me to marry him, and we're planning a Christmas wedding. Now there's a scoop for you! Dominic's going to make an honest woman of me at last.'

Jaime felt as if she couldn't breathe. 'You're having an affair?'

'Well, of course we're having an affair,' declared Catriona disparagingly. 'Honestly, Miss Harris, I thought I'd made that perfectly clear from the start.' She sighed, as if dealing with a rather backward child, and then continued patiently. 'Dominic's been my lover for years. He's crazy about me.'

Which was the moment when Jaime decided she had said enough. The idea of revealing her identity now, of telling this selfish, arrogant woman that she was her daughter, had suddenly become impossible. What did it matter, anyway? Catriona—Cathryn—had never wanted her when she was a child, so how likely was it that she'd want her now, as an adult?

Her coffee was getting cold, and although she had lost the taste for it Jaime forced herself to finish it off. After all, there was no point in wishing things could have been different. After what had happened between herself and Dominic, there was no way she and—Catriona could ever be friends.

CHAPTER FIFTEEN

DOMINIC stood at the window of his suite at the Ritz hotel looking out at the rain-soaked reaches of Green Park. Away to his left, Piccadilly ran down to Hyde Park Corner, while to his right was Piccadilly Circus, and the bustling heart of London's theatre district.

He often stayed at the Ritz when he was in London. Even though it was in the thriving centre of the city, it was an oasis of peace and civilisation. In addition to which, he was usually able to walk to most of his appointments. He'd soon discovered that driving around the nation's capital could be a frustrating experience.

Not that he'd be walking to his destination today. Notwithstanding the appalling weather, he had been given to understand that Chiswick was some distance from Piccadilly. Far enough, at any rate, to warrant leasing a hire car. A car that for once he intended to drive himself.

He expelled a long breath, trying to ease the sudden tightness in his shoulders. He was as tense as a cat and twice as jumpy. For God's sake, what if she refused to see him? Could he possibly have made this whole trip for nothing?

He sucked in another breath. He wouldn't believe that. Not that he hadn't had his doubts before he left. That was why he'd chosen not to warn her of his arrival. Anything she had to say to him, she could damn well say to his face.

And probably would, if he knew Jaime, he reflected ruefully. He had few illusions that seeing her again was going to solve his problems there and then. She already despised him for the way he'd treated her, and he had

159

the notion it was going to take more than a declaration of his feelings to persuade her he was sincere.

He sighed. If only she hadn't left like that. He'd had no idea when he'd gone to bed that night that she'd be gone when he woke up in the morning. Or that Catriona would be there, waiting for him, he appended sourly. His stepmother had been the last person he'd wanted to see...

'What do you mean Jaime's gone?' he'd demanded, at Catriona's arrogant words, and her eyes had narrowed at the familiarity his question implied.

'Just what I say,' she replied coolly, the thin smile on her lips not reaching her eyes. 'I'm sure you'd agree that she and I were never on the same wavelength, and when I saw the mess she'd made in my study I was incensed!'

'When did she leave?'

His response was clearly not what she'd expected, and although she must have sensed that all was not as it should be she was still prepared to give him the benefit of the doubt. 'I don't know,' she said. 'An hour—two hours ago. Does it matter? We shan't be seeing her again, if I have any say in the matter.'

'You don't.'

Dominic's lips flattened now as he recalled his bald statement. He remembered he'd even shocked himself with the certainty he'd heard in his voice. Without waiting for her to say anything more, he'd charged out of the house and leapt into the Toyota, heading for the airport to stop Jaime getting on the plane.

He'd been too late, of course. For reasons he could only guess at, Jaime hadn't waited for the evening flight. Instead, she'd apparently boarded one of the morning flights to the United States, either to prolong her visit or to find an alternative route back to London.

He guessed the latter. In her position, he would probably have taken the first flight off the island too. Had she suspected that he might come after her? Or had her eagerness to put an end to that unhappy chapter of her life been uppermost in her mind?

Whatever, he had had little opportunity to consider the matter. Catriona had been waiting for him when he'd got back to the house, and it had been immediately obvious from her expression that she was not going to be put off this time. As soon as he'd walked into the hall, she'd come to meet him, and for the first time he'd thought she looked her age.

'What the hell's going on?' she demanded, looking almost apprehensively past him, as if she expected Jaime to follow him into the house. 'Where on earth did you go rushing off to? I'd have followed you, if you hadn't taken the only car.'

Dominic scowled. 'I went to the airport, of course,' he retorted, far too frustrated himself to treat her with kid gloves. 'But, guess what? She wasn't there. What in God's name did you say to her? Why would she take a flight to the States instead of waiting for the evening flight to London?'

'She's gone?'

He didn't miss the look of relief that crossed her face at his response. 'Yeah, she's gone,' he confirmed, hooking his thumbs into the back pockets of his cut-offs. 'D'you want to tell me why?'

'I told you why, darling.' Now that she knew Jaime was gone, Catriona was evidently prepared to be generous. 'We didn't get on. I don't know what you're getting so het up about, sweetheart. It's not as if it's going to make any difference to you.'

Dominic took a deep breath. 'What if I say it is?'

Catriona stared at him. 'What?' Clearly, she chose to misunderstand his words.

'What if I say it does make a difference? To me,' he appended tersely. 'Will you ask her to come back if that's what I want?'

Catriona's expression underwent a series of changes,

and finally settled into a playful mask. 'Now, I know you don't mean that, darling,' she told him firmly. 'I'm sorry if you think I've been rather mean, but the woman irritated me. And I can't work with someone I don't even like.'

Dominic's lips tightened. 'Why didn't you like her?' he asked. 'She seemed perfectly—charming to me.'

'Well, she would.' Catriona's tone had sharpened. 'But she was just like Kristin. She was more interested in you than in her job.'

'In me?' Dominic stared at her. 'I don't believe it.'

'Oh, it's true.' Catriona was complacent. 'These women are all the same. They pretend to want the job, but what they really want is someone to pick up the tab.'

Dominic caught his breath. 'And that's why you fired her?'

'I fired her because she was presumptuous—among other things,' retorted Catriona, realising she was not making any headway on the other score. 'In any case, she agreed that we weren't suited to one another. I can assure you, she didn't hang around after I'd paid her off.'

Dominic's nostrils flared. 'And she didn't say—anything?'

'Anything about what?' Catriona was clearly beginning to think she had been tolerant enough. 'Dammit, Dom, what could she have said? We were never exactly friends.'

'No.' Dominic blew out a breath, and, moving past her, he walked into the sunlit living room. He halted before the windows. 'She didn't tell you what happened yesterday?' he queried over his shoulder. 'How I found her poking about in my room?'

'No!' Catriona followed him, her feelings showing in the angry exclamation she gave. 'In your room?' she echoed. 'My God, no, she didn't!' She paused. 'Did she know you were at home?'

Dominic grimaced, and then swung round. 'I guess

not,' he conceded drily. 'As a matter of fact, I scared the hell out of her.'

'But what was she doing?' Catriona was incensed. 'If she's stolen anything, I'll—'

'She hasn't.' Dominic's tone was flat now. 'And as a matter of fact she thought it was your room. She was unfamiliar with the layout of the house.'

'My room?' Catriona stared at him. 'But why would she want to go into my room?'

'She said she was looking for something,' replied Dominic smoothly. 'I thought you might be able to tell me what.'

Catriona looked taken aback now, and Dominic wondered what she was thinking as she paced across the floor. Obviously his words had disconcerted her, though she was doing her best to hide it, and he was hardly surprised when she didn't give him a direct answer.

'I hope you—chastised her,' she said at last. 'She had no right to go nosing about upstairs.' She took a breath. 'I think it proves my point when I said I didn't like her. I suspected she was an inquisitive creature and I was right.'

Dominic thrust his hands into his pockets. 'And you have no idea what she might have been looking for?'

'No.' Catriona's response was automatic, but after a moment she gave him a wary look. 'Why?' she asked. 'What did she say?' She paused. 'What has she been telling you? If she's been slandering me in my absence, I have a right to know.'

'What could she say?' Dominic lifted one shoulder in a dismissive shrug. 'I just wondered if—if you'd known her, before she came to work for you. There is a similarity between you. I mentioned it before.'

Catriona's gasp was audible. 'She has said something, hasn't she?' she exclaimed fiercely. 'That's what all this is about. She's been stringing you some sob story, and you believed her.'

Dominic went very still. 'Some sob story?' he echoed softly. 'What possible sob story could she have told me?'

'I don't know.' Catriona seemed to think better of confiding in him. 'It's just the way you're acting, darling.' She forced a laugh. 'You're making me feel as if I've done something wrong.'

'And have you?' Dominic's eyes were wary now.

'No.' Catriona held up her head. 'I don't know what all this is leading to, Dominic. If you've got something to say, why don't you spit it out?'

Dominic sighed, aware that he was only acting on instinct anyway. 'I've got nothing to say.'

'Good. Good.' Catriona made a concerted effort to recover her composure. 'That's all right, then, isn't it?' She sank down gracefully onto the sofa, and then patted the seat beside her. 'Come along. Sit down beside me. It seems so much longer than a week since you've been gone.'

Dominic made no move to join her. In all honesty, he was wondering what it was he had ever seen in her. She suddenly seemed so shallow, so selfish, so unfeeling; had the impression he'd conceived of her when he was just a boy blinded him to the woman he saw now, as a man?

'I have to get changed,' he said at last, realising he couldn't stay here, feeling as he did, and she uttered a cry of protest, before launching herself off the couch and into his arms.

'Oh, darling,' she breathed, wrapping her arms about his waist and pressing her face into his shoulder. 'Don't walk out on me now. I've missed you so much.'

'Cat—'

'Don't—don't say anything,' she whispered huskily. 'Just stay with me for a minute. I can't believe we'll soon be together for always. It seems forever since you held me in your arms.'

'Cat—' With a controlled effort, Dominic managed to hold her away from him. 'Cat, I don't know how to say this, but—I don't think you and I—have a future together.' He swallowed, aware of her horrified expression, but determined to go on regardless. 'I'm sorry. I know I'm letting you down, and I never intended that to happen. But—well, since my father died, things haven't been the same between us—'

'That's not true!' Catriona dragged herself away from him and gazed at him with disbelieving eyes. 'My God, not three weeks ago you were as frustrated by the situation as I was, only that misplaced loyalty you've always felt towards your father kept us apart.'

'No—'

'Yes.' She was positive. 'I don't believe this. I *won't* believe this. Something must have happened. You can't possibly have changed your mind without any cause.'

Dominic's sigh was heartfelt. 'Okay,' he said. 'Perhaps you're right. Perhaps something has happened. But it's not something I want to talk about. I just want you to understand how I feel.'

'It's her, isn't it?' Catriona's voice had risen now, and Dominic knew with a sense of doom that she was going to demand nothing less than the truth. Much as he might wish to avoid it, he was going to have to tell her of his feelings for Jaime. But they were so new and fragile, he was loath to lay them open to her hostile gaze.

'You don't understand—' he began, but Catriona didn't let him go on.

'Don't I? You underestimate me, Dominic. I think I'm beginning to understand only too well. It's Jaime, isn't it? You've let that woman poison your mind against me.'

Dominic groaned. 'Nobody's poisoned my mind, Catriona—'

'Haven't they?' She clenched her fists. 'Well, forgive me if I don't believe you. I knew she must have said something, but I never dreamt it would come to this.'

Dominic shook his head. 'Cat, listen to me—'

'No, you listen to me. She's a bitter woman, Dominic.

She's been brought up to believe I'm some kind of ogre, and now she's come here intent on seeking her revenge. She doesn't understand that what I did I did for all of us. If I'd stayed with Robert, I'd have probably gone mad!'

Dominic's lips parted. 'Robert?' he said, not immediately understanding what she was talking about. 'Who's Robert?'

'My first husband, of course,' cried Catriona frustratedly, twisting her hands together. 'Please don't insult me by telling me she didn't mention her father. Robert Michaels. I expect she told you that was her real name.'

Dominic was stunned. 'You mean—Jaime is your daughter?'

Catriona's lips curled. 'Don't pretend you didn't know.'

'I—didn't.' But his suspicions hadn't gone away despite what Jaime had said.

Catriona was not impressed. 'So what's all this about? You're telling me you're not breaking off our relationship because of what she told you?'

'Jaime told me nothing,' said Dominic heavily. 'Nothing to harm you, that is. And if you think the fact that you'd lied to me—and to my father, incidentally—would make a difference, think again.'

Catriona frowned. 'What do you mean?'

'I mean that if I still cared about you the knowledge that in the dim and distant past you were once married and had a child would mean next to nothing. I might have wondered why you'd chosen to keep it a secret, but I'm no angel, Cat. I know that people don't always behave in the way you'd want them to, and I'd have forgiven you. Dear God, if I was prepared to break up my marriage for you, I was hardly likely to kick up a fuss about you breaking yours. Get real, Cat; this has nothing to do with your unhappy past. It's to do with my future—mine—and Jaime's.'

'Yours and Jaime's!' Catriona stared at him in horror. 'For God's sake, Dominic, you barely know her!'

'I know her,' replied Dominic flatly, not prepared to go as far as to admit how well. 'I love her, Cat. I didn't know what love was until I met her. And I didn't know how much I wanted her until you said she'd gone.'

Catriona uttered an incredulous snort. 'I don't believe this.'

'Believe it.'

'But—' she spread her hands '—you've always told me you loved me.'

'I was wrong.' He spoke simply. 'I've realised all I really felt was infatuation: first, because I was an impressionable schoolboy, and then because you were someone I couldn't have.'

'But you could have had me!'

'I know.' His lips twisted. 'And haven't you ever wondered why I didn't take you? I don't suppose I'd have been able to keep you at arm's length all these months if I'd been as certain as you were that we were meant to be together.'

Catriona sneered. 'And is this what you told her?'

'Jaime? Yes, I guess so. She knows we've never been lovers. I explained that when my father died—'

'I told her we were lovers,' Catriona interrupted him maliciously, and smiled when she saw the look of consternation that crossed his face. She moved her shoulders reminiscently. 'We had quite a chat, she and I. Before the cab arrived to take her to the airport. I wondered if she'd have the nerve to confront me, now that she was leaving.'

Dominic felt frozen. 'How long have you known?'

'How long have I known what?'

'That Jaime is your daughter, of course.'

'Oh.' Catriona shrugged. 'Only since yesterday. I—I began to suspect she might be when you said she—looked a little like me. And Jaime isn't such a common name. But it was the resemblance that really bugged me. Personally, I couldn't see it, but I decided to check it out.'

Dominic's breath rushed out. 'You had her checked out? How?'

'A private detective, of course, darling. I could hardly go to England myself.'

'Was that why you decided to go to New York?'

'Oh, you sell yourself short, darling,' Catriona murmured, almost as if she was enjoying this now. 'I wanted to see you, naturally, so I decided to—kill two birds with one stone.'

'And your detective met you there.'

'He did. And, incidentally, turned up the fact that she's still employed by the university. She hasn't exactly been honest with either of us. She came here, under an assumed name, to poke her nose into my affairs.'

Dominic heaved a sigh. 'She had the right.'

'Did she?' Catriona obviously disagreed with him. 'Well, when I first found out, it may interest you to know that I was tempted to confront her, too. After all, she'd been living in my house, eating my food—'

'Doing her job,' put in Dominic harshly, but she ignored him.

'I was entitled to an explanation. I even wore this ring—the ring her father gave me,' she added, pointing to the small sapphire on her finger. 'I wanted to see if she had the guts to mention it.' Her lips curled. 'But she didn't.'

Dominic's jaw tightened. 'I've got to see her.'

'Why? So she can tell you to get lost in person?' Catriona uttered a mocking laugh. 'Admit it, Dom, she's never going to believe you now. I told her we were going to get married at Christmas, and I'm certainly not going to confess what an honourable fool you've been.'

A muscle in Dominic's cheek jerked, and he rubbed it almost absently. It was almost a week since he'd had that conversation with his stepmother, and most of that time had been spent trying to get his own affairs in order. Despite Catriona's pleas, he had insisted that he was going to England to find Jaime, and she had told him that if he did he would never enter her house again. She had also threatened to find another publisher, but Dominic could no longer live his life to her whim. If she left Goldman and Redding, they would have to bear it. With Thomas Aitken's name on their list, it might not be such a bad thing.

In consequence, he had spent the following few days moving all his belongings from the house at Copperhead Bay. While instinct had urged him to fly straight to London after Jaime, common sense had taught him that impulses could sometimes be wrong. Like him, she needed a breathing space. He refused to admit he was afraid to face her after what Catriona had said.

But he was here now, had been for a couple of days, in fact, checking out the university where she worked, discovering that she wasn't due back until the autumn term. He had her address; now he had to see her. He just prayed he could undo all the damage that Catriona's lying tongue had caused.

CHAPTER SIXTEEN

THE doorbell rang as Jaime was just stepping out of the shower. She'd spent the morning cleaning the house from top to bottom, and she'd decided to take a shower before meeting one of her university colleagues for lunch. She'd refused several invitations since she'd got back to England, but after a week of acting like a hermit she'd agreed to join Ian Hastings at the bistro the faculty members frequented near the college.

'Damn,' she said now, guessing it was probably one of her neighbours. Since her father died, the old lady next door had attempted to take Jaime under her wing. She was forever calling round with newly baked pies or cakes she professed to have no use for, and, while Jaime appreciated her kindness, it was a little overpowering sometimes.

The doorbell rang again, and, realising Mrs Napier knew she was at home, and would probably think she was avoiding her if she didn't answer, Jaime wrapped her shabby pink bathrobe about her and started down the stairs, tying the cord as she went. She just hoped Mrs Napier wouldn't insist on putting whatever it was she'd brought away in the fridge. There were already the remains of two pies she'd given her earlier in the week occupying one of the shelves.

'Sorry,' she was saying as she opened the door, aware of the wet tangle of her hair dripping down her neck. 'I was just getting out of the shower when...'

'How appropriate!'

Jaime could only stare at him. The apologetic words trailed away into an uncomfortable silence, and she was instantly aware of what a sight she must look. But then, she thought wryly, what did it matter? He hadn't come here to admire her doubtful charms.

But why had he come?

'Aren't you going to invite me in?'

His words were confident enough, but there was a kind of clipped edge to his voice, as if he wasn't exactly sure how to play this. And why not, after the way he had lied to her? Could it conceivably be Catriona who had sent him to turn the screw?

'I don't think so,' she said, managing to sound almost pleasant. 'As you can see, I was just taking a shower, and I'm going out in fifteen minutes, so—'

'Please.'

His dark eyes held hers in mute persuasion, and she could feel herself weakening by the second. Oh, God, she thought, why had he had to come here now, just when she was beginning to feel half normal? It was cruel; she'd hoped she'd never have to see him again.

'What do you want, Dominic?' she asked, deciding she'd never get another moment's peace if she sent him away without finding out. It was all very well telling herself she should just close the door in his face. But she knew she'd regret it later, when she'd had time to think.

'We can't talk on the doorstep,' he said. 'Apart from anything else, you're getting cold.' He gestured at the rain that was soaking the shoulders of his leather jacket. 'So am I.'

Jaime pressed her lips together. 'I didn't ask you to come here.'

'I know that.' He sighed. 'But I couldn't stay away.' He paused. 'Jaime, please—I've got to talk to you. At least have the courtesy to hear what I have to say.'

The words, Why should I? trembled on Jaime's lips, but they were never spoken. Instead, with a resigned shake of her shoulders, she moved aside, and he stepped heavily into the hall.

Immediately, the narrow passageway seemed crowded, and Jaime hurriedly closed the door before gesturing for him to go into the front room. 'I won't be a minute,' she said, her fingers curling tightly over the baluster. 'Help yourself to a drink while I get dressed.'

He looked as if he might protest, but evidently discretion—and common sense—had their way. 'Thank you,' he said, and she nodded before starting up the stairs.

She was half afraid he might follow her. All the time she was towelling her hair, putting on her underwear, donning a pair of leggings and a baggy sweater, she was listening with some apprehension for his footsteps on the stairs. But she achieved her objective without any interruption, and, deciding she couldn't wait to use the handdrier on her hair, she contented herself with wrapping it up in a towel.

Downstairs again, she found Dominic where she had directed him. He was standing by the sitting-room window, staring out at the persistent rain. He hadn't helped himself to a drink; his hands were pushed into his pockets, and when he heard her somewhat nervous entrance he swung round to give her a guarded smile.

'An English summer,' he said wryly. 'No wonder everywhere always looks so green.'

'We're used to it,' said Jaime tersely. 'Have you been in England long? Is—is Catriona with you?'

She was trying to be polite, trying to behave as if his appearance on her doorstep were no big thing, and that her departure from her employment had been achieved without any duress. She had no idea what Catriona might have told him, but no expectation that her role in the proceedings had been given a friendly press. He probably thought she'd run away because she was afraid of him. Even if that was partly true, he would never hear it from her lips.

'No,' Dominic replied now, his mouth tightening slightly, and she wondered if he didn't like being reminded of his responsibilities in this way. If he'd come alone, he might have some notion that they could continue their association. Now that she was away from his stepmother's influence, it was possible he was conceited enough to think she might welcome his attentions.

The breath caught in her throat. *As if.*

'I came alone,' Dominic continued, and she sensed that he was nervous too. 'I flew in a couple of days ago. I'm staying at the Ritz.'

'How nice.' Jaime managed to keep any feelings she might have out of her voice. 'Are you staying long?'

'Do you care?'

The roughness of his enquiry caught her unawares, and for a moment she gazed at him with disbelieving eyes. But then prudence, and irritation at her own naivety, brought a swift return of sanity, and she grasped the back of a chair for support.

'Look,' she said, when it became obvious he was waiting for a reply, 'I don't know why you've come here, but if it's anything to do with what happened in Bermuda—'

'Of course it is,' he interrupted her impatiently. 'And before you start telling me that what happened didn't mean anything to you I want you to know that it meant a hell of a lot to me.'

'Oh, yes?' She didn't believe him.

'Yes.'

'Was that before or after Catriona found out what happened?' Jaime demanded bitterly. 'I assume that is how it worked, isn't it? That's the real reason you're here.'

'No, damn you, it's not,' he returned hotly. 'Hell, that's some opinion of me you've got there. Maybe I am wasting my time, after all.'

'Maybe you are.' Jaime breathed deeply. 'Catriona does know what happened, doesn't she?'

'Not from me,' replied Dominic grimly. 'I can't speak for you, of course.'

'Me?' Jaime gasped. 'I didn't tell her anything.'

'Right.' His face was bitter now. 'You didn't even try to find out if she was your mother. Well, I've got news for you: she is.'

Jaime sighed. 'I know that.'

'You know?'

'Of course.' Jaime shook her head, and then wished she hadn't when the towel slipped down around her ears. She pulled it off, and felt the damp strands of hair slipping softly over her shoulders. 'Look—maybe I haven't been completely honest with you. I—I was fairly sure—Catriona was who I thought she was before I left England.'

'But you said—'

'I know what I said.' Jaime flushed.

Dominic stared at her. 'So you didn't just base your suspicions on her photograph like you said?'

Jaime bit her lip. 'Well—I did have a photograph,' she admitted unwillingly. 'But it wasn't on the back of her books. I found it in my father's belongings when he died.'

'A photograph of Catriona?'

'And—and my father.' Jaime nodded unhappily. 'As well as some clippings he'd collected from newspaper interviews she had given over the years.'

'So you knew she was your mother right from the start?'

'Pretty much.' Jaime was loath to admit how full of hope and anticipation she'd been when she'd left London. 'I wanted to get to know her for myself. My father—well, my father was biased, I suppose, and I needed to find out if—if he was wrong.'

'And was he?'

'I don't know.'

Jaime couldn't condemn Catriona even now. She had no way of knowing the kind of life her mother had led with her father. She had been much too young. And perhaps success had spoilt Catriona. She would never know.

'Anyway,' she said now, realising that she had misjudged him, too, 'if that's why you came here, then I'm sorry you've had a wasted journey.'

'Have I?' Dominic pulled his hands out of his pockets and raked slightly unsteady fingers through his hair. 'You don't even know why I'm here yet.'

'But I thought—'

'That I'd come to put the record straight?' he asked, his eyes dark and intent. 'Well, I guess I did, in a manner of speaking. But not just for Cat's sake. For my own as well.'

'She—she knows you're here?'

Jaime felt a hollowness in the pit of her stomach. Just because Catriona wasn't with him, that didn't mean she hadn't given him her blessing.

'I'd say she has a pretty good idea,' he declared drily, one hand coming to rest at the nape of his neck. He made a rueful sound. 'She was fairly vehement about my choice of destination, of course, but I think she knew I was unlikely to take her advice.'

Jaime swallowed. 'I don't know what you mean.'

'Do the words "Go to hell" sound familiar?'

Jaime pressed a hand to her mouth. 'You don't mean that.'

'Don't I?' He was sardonic. 'That's not the way I see it.'

'But—she said—'

'Yes? What did she say? I'd like to know.'

Jaime licked her lips. 'Well—that you'd asked her to marry you at—at Christmas.'

'I see.'

'Isn't it true?' Jaime held her breath.

Dominic's hand dropped to his side. 'If I'm honest I'll have to admit that I did once suggest that we might get married at Christmas,' he agreed, and Jaime's heart did a painful flop. 'But in my own defence I have to say I agreed to it just to get her off my back.'

Jaime lifted her head. 'How could you do that?'

'How?' His lips twisted. 'I suppose I have to say it seemed a good idea at the time. After what happened that afternoon on the yacht, I guess I was in a state of denial. I'd have said anything to prove to myself that nothing had changed.'

'So you gave in to her?'

Even as she asked the question, Jaime wondered why she was bothering to go on with this. He'd admitted he'd asked her mother to marry him, and if Catriona hadn't been lying about that, then obviously she hadn't been lying about their being lovers either.

'Yeah.' Dominic gazed at her with defeated eyes. 'I gave in to her.'

'Like you've been giving in to her all along,' said Jaime scornfully. 'Exactly when did you make her your mistress? Was that before or after your father died?'

Dominic swore. 'God,' he said. 'You don't pull your punches, do you?'

Jaime was trembling. 'Not when I've been lied to.'

'I haven't lied to you.' Dominic's eyes were dark with a mixture of anger and pain. 'Believe it or not, I've never slept with Catriona. Not because I haven't wanted to on occasion, and not because I haven't had the opportunity. I have. Plenty of times. But something—I don't know what—has always stopped me from committing myself that far.' His lips twisted. 'Perhaps I always knew there was something better waiting just around the corner.'

Jaime took a backward step. 'I hope you're not going to pretend that's me.'

'Why not?'

'Why not?' She gave a hysterical little sob. 'Dominic, I know I'm not as sophisticated as—as Catriona, but even I can recognise a line when I hear one.'

Dominic looked weary suddenly. 'And that's what you think this is?'

'Well, what else am I supposed to think?' she demanded. 'You—you come on to me, then you—you—'

'Seduce you?' he suggested bitterly, and she seized on his words.

'Yes. Seduce me,' she added breathily. 'And I—I don't remember any great declarations of intent.'

'That's because there was so much else going on besides,' said Dominic harshly. 'First of all, I thought you were checking the place out in Cat's absence, and then you got so mad, you almost told me the truth. I say *almost*. You reneged on that as soon as you'd had time to think.'

'It wasn't up to me to tell you.' She frowned suddenly. 'Did you tell—Catriona what you suspected?'

Dominic regarded her anxious face with sardonic eyes. 'I didn't have to. I was still trying to find a way to break it to her that our association—hers and mine— was over, and she got it into her head that you'd told me about your relationship with her.'

'Oh, God!' Jaime felt terrible. 'And had she known all along who—I was?'

'No. That's why she went to New York. She'd had a private detective agency check you out. I don't know if she planned to confront you, or what. I guess my being at the house baulked her plans a little.'

'Oh, God,' said Jaime again, but Dominic was philosophical about the whole thing.

'It doesn't matter. It wasn't important,' he told her softly. 'I just wanted you to know the way it was.'

Jaime looked stunned. 'I can't believe this.'

'I know what you mean.' Dominic's lips twisted. 'I didn't want to believe it, either. Dammit, Jaime, I've

spent the last twenty years telling myself that it was
Catriona I loved, Catriona I wanted. It isn't easy realising that what you felt—what you thought you'd been
feeling—was just—infatuation.'

Jaime pushed her damp hair off her forehead. 'But
how do you know it was?'

'Because I've now experienced the real thing,' he told
her savagely. 'For pity's sake, Jaime, why the hell do
you think I've come here?'

'I thought you'd come to tell me about my mother.'

'That too.' Dominic groaned. 'But you know that
wasn't the only reason.'

Jaime couldn't accept this. 'And—and it was when
you found out that Catriona was my mother that—that
you and she—split up?' she asked tensely, and Dominic
covered the floor between them in a couple of strides.

'Haven't you been listening to a word I've said?' he
snarled, grasping her shoulders. 'Why would I give a
damn about what Catriona did before she married my
father? She's a grown woman, for God's sake. She could
have had half a dozen husbands and I wouldn't have
cared. Right?'

Jaime quivered. 'If you say so.' He'd never hear that
Catriona was older than she claimed from her.

'I do say so.' His hands gentled. 'I guess what I find
a little hard to come to terms with is the fact that you
let her get away with it. But that's your decision, not
mine.'

Jaime sniffed. 'Get away with—with what?'

'With deserting you and your father. With ignoring
the young woman you grew up to be.' He shrugged.
'Still, I guess that's her misfortune, hmm?'

Jaime bent her head, feeling the tears suddenly pricking the backs of her eyes. 'She had her reasons.'

'Yeah, right. And they were all selfish ones,' said
Dominic flatly. 'Oh, Jaime, can we talk about us? Have

you any idea how I felt when I found you'd walked out on me?'

Jaime shook her head, hardly able to think of anything with his fingers gripping her shoulders and the scent of damp leather and warm flesh filling her nostrils. 'I—I didn't walk out on you,' she managed at last, and his thumbs came to tip her face up to his.

'It certainly looked like it,' he said softly, his eyes gentler than she'd ever seen them. 'Tell me, what else did Cat say?'

'Oh—you know,' Jaime whispered huskily. 'She told me what I said—about you being lovers, and getting married at Christmas.'

'What else?'

'Well, that she and I weren't compatible, and that it would be best for all concerned if I left.'

Dominic uttered a harsh word. 'So you did.'

'Yes.'

'Even though you knew I didn't want you to go.'

'You'd said you didn't want me to leave until—until Catriona got back. Well, she was back, and—'

'You decided you'd had enough?'

'Pretty much,' said Jaime tremulously, and then caught her breath when he bent his head and stroked her lips with his tongue. 'Dominic, please. You don't have to do this.'

'Oh, I do.' She heard the tremor in his voice, and quivered in spite of herself. 'I'm not just having to come to terms with my feelings for Catriona; I'm also having to accept that I'm in great danger of ruining the only real relationship I've ever known.'

'Dominic—'

'I like the way you say my name.' His fingers came to cup her face, his thumbs rubbing sensuously over her lower lip. 'God, Jaime, do you have any idea how frightened I was before I came here? I was afraid you wouldn't see me, wouldn't speak to me, wouldn't let me explain. It would have been so easy for you to tell me to get lost. Goodness knows, it's what I probably deserve.'

Jaime drew a trembling breath. 'I wouldn't do that.'

'No.' His mouth compressed. 'You're far more tolerant than me. After the way I treated you, the night before you left, I was sure you wouldn't believe what I had to say.'

Jaime caught her lower lip between her teeth, tasting the flavour of his flesh on her tongue. 'You were angry—'

'I was frustrated,' he amended flatly. 'I knew what I was feeling, but I wasn't prepared to accept it. I couldn't accept it. I thought as soon as Cat came back I'd get things into perspective—and I did. Only not in the way I planned. When she told me you'd gone—' He shook his head. 'I don't know who I blamed most: you or me.'

Jaime was finding it hard to take this in. 'But you knew where I'd gone.'

'I thought I did.' His fingers stroked the sensitive skin below her ear. 'I assumed you'd gone to the airport, so I hightailed it across to St George's so fast I broke every rule in the book. Only I was too late. You'd left the island.'

Jaime frowned. 'When was this?'

'About lunchtime that day.' He grimaced. 'I slept in, okay? I could say it was your fault that I'd sunk almost a whole bottle of Scotch before I could get to sleep the night before, but that wouldn't be fair, would it? Even if it's true.' His eyes softened. 'Let's just say I got stoned, and by the time I dragged my miserable carcass downstairs Catriona was primed and waiting for me.'

Jaime didn't want to think about that. 'I—I flew to the States,' she said, trying to ignore the heated awareness that was communicating itself through the sensuous touch of his hands. 'To—to Atlanta.'

'Yeah. I guessed.' His eyes darkened. 'I'd probably have done the same in your position.'

Jaime hesitated. 'Will—will she forgive you?'

'Cat?' Dominic's brows drew together. 'I suppose that depends on how much I want to be forgiven,' he replied tautly, and she gave him a puzzled look.

'I don't understand.'

'You should.' His hands slid into the wet coils of her hair and drew her closer—so close she could feel the faint tremor in his body. 'I love you, Jaime,' he said huskily. 'And I want us to be together. And if, as a part of that, you want me to make my peace with Catriona...' he lifted his shoulders '...I will.'

Jaime was trembling now. 'Oh, Dominic...'

'Oh, Jaime,' he mimicked softly. Then he said, 'Will you forgive me? That's the most important thing. Anything else is pure indulgence...'

CHAPTER SEVENTEEN

JAIME stepped into the shower cubicle and gulped at the sudden coolness of the water against her hot skin. But there was no emotional chill, no sense of dismay or guilt at what they had done, and her senses still quivered with the sensual images that filled her inner vision. She was in love, she thought incredulously, and it was everything and more than she'd believed it could be.

'Dominic...'

His name slipped from her lips, and she had to hug herself to contain the sense of excitement she felt at knowing he loved her too. It didn't seem possible that one person could be so happy, and she tilted her face to the refreshing spray, allowing the cooling stream of water to wash the heat of sweat—and sex—from her body.

Dominic was still asleep. She'd left him tangled in the sheets, his lean face relaxed and looking younger than she ever remembered seeing him. He was exhausted, she thought ruefully, recalling the urgency of their love-making with a renewed need. The fever he had aroused in her refused to be assuaged, and she ran her hands down over her breasts and her abdomen to the aching muscles of her thighs.

She had thought after that first time that it couldn't get any better, but it had. Every time he'd made love to her, every time he'd parted her thighs and came into her, her mind splintered with the urgent needs he created. She'd wanted him; she'd wanted all of him, and when she'd wrapped her legs about his hips she'd been showing him how much.

There had been times, she acknowledged now, when

she hadn't recognised herself in the primitive woman she'd become. She hadn't believed she was the kind of woman who would react so violently to his demands. Before Dominic, no man had ever touched that special place inside her, and his wants and his needs had become as important to her as her own.

But then, Dominic was something special, she admitted with a little shiver. And he seemed to have an instinctive understanding of her body. His lovemaking had been hard and fast at times, but through it all she'd been aware of his gentleness, and his generosity, and although he had been hot and eager for his own release he'd kept a tight rein on his emotions.

All the same, there'd been times when she'd seen the strain he was putting on himself in his face. Times when the muscles had corded in his neck, and a sheen of sweat had coated his throat. But then he'd looked down at her, and she'd seen the tenderness enter his eyes, the sensuality curl his mouth in an expression she was growing to know so well.

If sex was power, then so was love, she thought whimsically. It was love that had brought Dominic to England, and love that had compelled her to invite him into her bed...

She expelled a tremulous breath, and then started violently when a hand curved possessively about her waist. She had been so wrapped up in her thoughts, she hadn't been aware of the glass door opening, and she glanced round to find Dominic stepping into the cubicle behind her.

'Why didn't you wake me?' he asked, drawing her back against him, and she was once again gripped by the sensual excitement he could so easily engender.

'I didn't want to disturb you,' she said unevenly, aware of how inappropriate her words were when he was so obviously disturbed. The powerful heat of his body swelled against her thighs, and the mouth he turned against her nape was hot and hungry.

'An impossible task,' he breathed, his hands curving over her breasts, and she felt their tenderness cradled against his palms. He had suckled at them earlier, and they were still sore and swollen. 'You always disturb me.'

Jaime drew a breath and tipped her head back against his shoulder. 'Do you mind?'

'Stop fishing,' he ordered softly, drawing her hands down the sides of his thighs. 'Just tell me why you need a shower right now. I can think of much better things to do.'

'It's half past four,' she protested. 'We have to eat.'

'Why?' He uttered a soft laugh. 'I have eaten.' He paused. 'You.'

She quivered. 'That's not what I mean.'

'No, I guess not.' He left her hands at his sides and returned to caressing her breasts. 'Okay. Where's the soap? I'll help you.'

Jaime's breath caught in her throat. 'You can't—'

'Why can't I?' He flipped the carton of shower gel out of her grasp, and began to lave her stomach with some of the slippery substance. 'See: I make a pretty good job of it.'

'No, you don't.' Jaime could feel her own arousal causing a trembling in her legs. 'Dominic...' She turned to face him. 'Dominic...'

It was a mistake. The feel of his manhood probing that place between her legs sent all thoughts of reasoning with him out of her head. Looking at him, looking into his eyes, she was lost, and she could only wind her arms tightly around his neck as he lifted her against him.

He drove into her fiercely, and she wrapped her legs about his waist and gave herself over to the incredible feelings he was inspiring inside her. She loved him, loved him so completely that nothing else mattered.

Whatever the future held, she would always have these moments to remember...

An hour later, Dominic and Jaime faced one another across the breakfast bar in the kitchen. Despite his reluctance to leave the comfort of her bed, Dominic had eventually had to admit to being hungry, and Jaime had rustled up an impromptu meal of steaks and salad. They were now lingering over the remains of the bottle of hock she had found in the fridge, Jaime in her old pink bathrobe, and Dominic wearing a navy silk kimono she had admitted to once buying for her father. The fact that he had never worn it wasn't so surprising. Judging from what Jaime had told him about her father over the simple meal, Dominic guessed he hadn't been the kind of man to wear something so extravagant. It wasn't really his choice either, but it was far more intimate than his damp jeans and sweatshirt.

And he found he liked that word—intimate. Being here with Jaime, in her own surroundings, so to speak, he felt amazingly content, and he realised he hadn't felt at home anywhere for an awfully long time. When his father was alive, he used to kid himself he was at home at Copperhead Bay, but the truth was, once Catriona had taken up residence, it had never been his home.

For a brief time, during his short marriage, he'd known a temporary kind of contentment, but it hadn't lasted. His feelings for Mary Beth had never stood a chance against the kind of influence Catriona had exerted, and it was only now that he was beginning to realise how futile that relationship had been.

His love for Jaime was of a whole different order. He could even feel sorry for Catriona now. He doubted she had ever known the strength of emotion he felt for her daughter. Her needs were all about control. She took, but she didn't give anything in return, whereas Jaime...

His eyes gentled as they rested on the woman he loved

so much he couldn't imagine now how empty his life had been without her. She had so much to give, and he intended to be there to share that giving with her.

'So tell me about what you do at the university,' he said, wanting to know all there was to know about her. 'Do you teach?'

'English,' agreed Jaime, with a wry grimace. 'It's not very exciting, but it pays the bills.'

'And you lived here with your father?'

'Until he died,' she nodded. 'He had cancer, you see. My grandmother was always grumbling at him because he smoked so much.'

'I see.' Dominic was thoughtful. 'And when he died you discovered all this stuff about Catriona?'

'About—Cathryn,' said Jaime ruefully. 'That was my mother's name before she—before she left home. Cathryn Michaels, who became Catriona Markham. Then Catriona Redding when she married your father.'

Dominic nodded. 'So—when were they divorced?'

Jaime flushed. 'I don't know.'

'You don't know?' He frowned. 'But weren't the papers with your father's belongings? They're the sort of things people tend to keep. I should know.'

Jaime looked at him. 'You were married?'

'For a brief time, when I was in my early twenties,' he admitted drily. 'But Catriona didn't like her, for obvious reasons, and the marriage broke up.'

Jaime moistened her lips. 'Did you love her?'

'Who? Mary Beth?' Dominic considered for a moment. 'I was very fond of her,' he said at last. 'But my association with Catriona made any kind of normal relationship impossible to sustain, and without involving my father there was nothing I could do.' He grimaced. 'I guess that sounds as though I'm blaming Dad, and I'm not. But if he'd ever guessed why Catriona had taken such an immediate dislike to Mary Beth he'd have been very hurt.'

'Have you seen her again?'

'Mary Beth?' he asked again. 'Yes, as it happens, I have. She eventually remarried—an old college friend, as a matter of fact. I believe they have a couple of children now. She's much happier with him than she ever was with me.'

Jaime took a breath. 'And you don't regret it?'

'Regret what? That my marriage broke up, or the fact that it's taken me so long to realise what a fool I've been?' He blew out a rueful breath. 'If I'm honest, I have to say my marriage to Mary Beth never stood a chance. I was too young, too immature, and in some ways I only married her as a kind of defence against my attraction to Catriona.' His eyes darkened. 'Still, if I hadn't behaved as I did, I'd never have met you. I guess I always knew there was something missing in my relationships with both Mary Beth and Catriona, but until you came along I didn't know what it was.'

Jaime coloured becomingly. 'So long as you're sure.'

'Do you doubt it?' Dominic put his hand across the table and linked his fingers with hers. 'I've never been so sure of anything in my life. I love you, Jaime. I want to marry you. Does that answer your question?'

Jaime breathed a little unevenly. 'I love you, too.'

Dominic's grip tightened. 'That's good. But don't look at me like that.' His eyes twinkled. 'It's not good to be too energetic on a full stomach.'

Jaime laughed then, and although he wanted her very much at that moment Dominic forced himself to be sensible. 'So...' he said. 'You don't know when your parents got divorced?'

'No.' Jaime looked doubtful now. 'I don't honestly know if Catriona ever contacted my father again. If she had, I'm sure my grandmother would have known about it, and she didn't say anything to me.'

'Ah.'

Dominic was intrigued. It had occurred to him that if

Catriona hadn't divorced her first husband her marriage
to Lawrence Redding should never have taken place. In
any event, in those circumstances it was invalid, and the
will his father had left was invalid also.

'What's wrong?'

Jaime was looking anxious now, and Dominic
squeezed her fingers again before replying. 'I was just
thinking how awkward it could be for Catriona if she
had never got a divorce. Not least because of what she
inherited as my father's widow.'

'Oh, I see.' Jaime stared at him. 'What are you going
to do?'

Dominic was silent for so long, she was beginning to
wonder if he had heard her, but then, at last, he drawled
his reply. 'Nothing,' he said softly. 'I'm going to do
nothing. But if Catriona goes through with her threat to
leave Goldman and Redding—' he smiled '—I may just
make some enquiries of my own...'

Jaime and Dominic were married six weeks later.

They got married at a small church in Chiswick, with
few guests other than Jaime's colleagues from the university. A couple of Dominic's friends flew over for the
ceremony, and Sophie and Samuel were there, much to
Jaime's surprise.

'Sophie always had a soft spot for me,' relayed
Dominic smugly. 'She's always resented the way
Catriona interfered in my life.'

Jaime's eyes widened. 'So why did she always treat
me as if I wasn't welcome?' she asked curiously, and
Dominic bent to give her a teasing kiss.

'I suppose because she had had high hopes for
Kristin,' he replied, laughing. 'She obviously thought
that you weren't my type.'

Jaime squeezed the arm she had linked with hers.
'And here was I thinking she was Catriona's ally. I won-

dered why she was so amenable the night before I left
the island.'

'I guess she thought you'd cracked it,' remarked
Dominic lazily. 'You know you've got her blessing at
least.'

They spent their honeymoon in Hawaii—three weeks
of relaxing and soaking up the sun on Kauai, the garden
island. Their hotel was small and luxurious, off the usual
tourist track, and perfect for two people to be alone.

Jaime didn't return to her job at the London university. She was lucky enough to acquire a temporary post
at a college in New York, and she and Dominic started
house-hunting on Long Island. For the time being, they
were quite content to share Dominic's duplex in
Manhattan, and Jaime blossomed in the glory of his love.

Catriona never did leave Goldman and Redding.

A formal letter announcing her intention not to do so
followed the congratulatory fax she sent to her daughter
and son-in-law when their first child was born. She had
abandoned the contemporary novel she had been writing
in favour of another historical, she declared. She had
recognised her limitations, she added ambiguously, and
she hoped the association would go on for many years
yet.

'It's a beginning, I suppose,' said Jaime softly, when
Dominic brought the communication to her, and her husband gave her a wry smile.

'Some day,' he said, admiring his new daughter,
'some day, she's going to want to be a grandmother. But
for now I'd like to keep both of you to myself.'

HARLEQUIN ✦ PRESENTS®

Indulge yourself in our spectacular
selection of top authors:

Sandra Marton
Romantic Times gold medal winner
August 1997—THE SECOND MRS ADAMS #1899

Helen Bianchin
"...tantalizing sexual tension."
—*Romantic Times*
September 1997—AN IDEAL MARRIAGE? #1905

Anne Mather
New York Times bestselling author,
with over 60 million books in print
October 1997—SHATTERED ILLUSIONS #1911

Available wherever Harlequin books are sold.

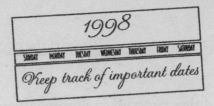

1998

| SUNDAY | MONDAY | TUESDAY | WEDNESDAY | THURSDAY | FRIDAY | SATURDAY |

Keep track of important dates

Three beautiful and colorful calendars that celebrate some of the most popular trends in America today.

Look for:

Just Babies—a 16 month calendar that features a full year of absolutely adorable babies!

1998 CALENDAR
Just Babies
16 months of adorable bundles of joy!

Hometown Quilts—a 16 month calendar featuring quilted art squares, plus a short history on twelve different quilt patterns.

Hometown Quilts
1998 Calendar
A 16 month quilting extravaganza!

Inspirations—a 16 month calendar with inspiring pictures and quotations.

Inspirations
A 16 month calendar that will lift your spirits and gladden your heart

Steeple Hill™

HARLEQUIN®

Value priced at $9.99 U.S./$11.99 CAN., these calendars make a perfect gift!

Available in retail outlets in August 1997.   CAL98